HARD MEN!

Cowley looked up. He saw a tall, slim black man impeccably dressed but who looked a little the worse for wear. He reeled into the office, and then halted, as though worked with wires. Bodie and Doyle stepped in. They smiled.

Cowley said, 'The pimp?'

'Henry Aloysius Wences. Take a seat, Aloysius,' said Bodie.

Wences sat down and glared around.

'This is not a regular bust. You're not coppers!'

'No,' Cowley told him. 'We're much worse . . .'

Also by Ken Blake in Sphere Books:

THE PROFESSIONALS 2:
Long Shot

KEN BLAKE

Based on the original screenplays by
Brian Clemens, Anthony Read and
P. J. Hammond

SPHERE BOOKS LTD.
30/32 Gray's Inn Road, London WC1X 8JL

First published in Sphere Books 1978
This novelisation Copyright © Sphere Books Ltd 1978
Reprinted 1978 (twice)

Set in Intertype Baskerville

Printed in Great Britain by
Hunt Barnard Printing Ltd,
Aylesbury, Bucks

Chapter One

The day burned hot. It was hotter still down in the concrete slot of the two-lane approach road to the tunnel sliced out of riverine clay. Concrete road surfaces, concrete buttresses and walls, concrete ramps and overbridges. The heat reflected back with the virulence of an out-of-control sauna, drenching everyone in perspiration. The air hung blue with carbon-monoxide and exhaust gases, the stink raw and grating on lip and tongue, irritating eyes. The cars and lorries crawled towards the black oval mouth of the tunnel, and halted, and inched on, and stopped once more.

Transistor radios blared from wound-down lorry windows, children cried, dogs barked, the eternal growling, churning of a hundred engines revving and dragging vehicles a few yards, blended into an unholy racket laced with the stink of hot rubber and petrol fumes. The ivory-tower planners' dream of twentieth-century road travel had turned into a motorists' nightmare.

Jammed in among the slowly-moving queue of cars and vans a blue-painted security van inched along. Immediately in its rear a tarted-up sports saloon dragged on, all its 'go-faster' accessories and motoring kitsh absurd in that bottom-gear jerking crawl.

Gerald Lewis with his bare left forearm resting on the leather-covered wheel and his right hanging out of the open window felt the sweat prickling all over him. His son, young Ronald, kept on and on, and his wife, Rosie, practically fainting in the heat and stink, sat slumped, uselessly, at his side. Young Ronald, almost thirteen, wanted to know everything. Now, he kept on about the security van up ahead, whose small, mesh-guarded rear windows glared back blankly at them from up front.

'So how,' said young Ronald, 'do they get the money out, Dad?'

'I don't know.'

'But, Dad, if the man stays in the back . . . Dad, how?'

'There's a door in the side – I don't know.' Lewis leaned out of the window. 'Oh, come on! Come on!'

Back in the queue Mr and Mrs Bilston – who had achieved that blissful state at eleven o'clock this morning – sat in their Mini holding hands whenever the car stopped. In this start and stop progress their sweaty hands touched to cling and part. Every now and then a fresh brightly-coloured piece of confetti turned up, and they'd laugh. But, all the same, this hold-up for the tunnel made Jack Bilston think he was being cheated, being delayed in the vital consummation he planned. Brenda shared his view. He stroked his left hand down her thigh, over the flower-patterned dress, and then back, and she smiled happily and leaned against him. Now they were really married it was All Right.

Thoroughly fed-up with this nonsense, Jack Bilston leaned out of the window to look ahead where yellow and red road marker cones showed up brightly in the sunshine. The lumbering, prehistoric-monster shapes of earth-moving machinery bulked against the concrete.

'What is it, darling?'

'Roadworks up ahead. This is going to take hours!'

The powerful streamlined Rover 3500 towing the four-wheel caravan inched along with all the other jammed vehicles. Tom Sumner sat watching his wife using a little battery-powered fan to move perhaps ten cc's of overheated air around. The sun burned into the car, the caravan jolted along at the back, the smell of overheated metal and tar and rubber reached in. He'd served in the Marines out in some pretty ferociously hot places; but this caper looked as

6

though it would beat the lot. He was making good money now with the firm as a sales executive, money he could have done with a few years ago. But he'd made up his mind to spend it whilst he had it. He kept in shape, did his daily dozen, and no Canadian Air Force nonsense, either. A Royal Marine knew how to keep fit, even if he was pushing along and sprouting a few grey hairs along his temples.

'I thought we'd get a quick run to the coast,' said Mary, his wife, waving the silly little fan about. 'But this is dreadful.'

'Road works,' said Sumner. 'On a week-day! Now why can't they mend their lousy roads on a Sunday?'

Up ahead the two lanes narrowed into one. Blue and white arrowmarkers diverted the outside lane to the inner. Cars were inching across with their winkers flashing, and the inside lane gave way or did not give way. Tempers were on a short fuse all the way along the line of sweating, irritable drivers. The reek of diesel fumes and the tongue-coating stinks of a motor-age jam in that suffocating slot brought the bile dangerously close to the surface. Overhead, as though mocking the log-jam below, cars sped across the overpasses, free, released, the clean air whipping past their windscreens.

The Hillman Avenger Estate with the wire mesh screen separating off the driver from the rear deck churned along in the line. The driver, somewhat elderly but not realising it yet, turned to look through the mesh at the two Labradors whose tongues hung out like Monday's washing in the heat.

'Good lad, Toby,' said Terence Lansbury, in his soft voice. 'All right, then, Girl.'

The dogs regarded him with their great eyes moist and patient. They panted gently. Lansbury looked back to take up his patient crawling progress.

The new but already dented Bedford van with the bright yellow paint job grunted along in bottom and, then like all the other vehicles, lurched to a standstill. Bert Williams listened to Radio One and beat in time on the steering wheel

7

as his mate, young Alf Hardstaff, leafed for the umpteenth time through the day's *Sun*, returning more often than not to page three. The Bedford churned along in the slot of heat.

Of them all in the queue perhaps only George Smiley could take the hold-up in his stride. He drove his lorry all day and every day, as far and as fast as traffic regulations would allow. Now he listened to the radio, the pop tunes barely registering, chewing on a nutty bar, letting his big arctic roll on with the utmost economy of effort.

You might trundle down the M.1 like a streak of blue lightning; but Smiley knew when you hit the smoke you fitted in like a pea in a pod and took your turn. Mind you, if any idiot wanted to squeeze a snazzy sports coupé in front of the massive artic, George Smiley wasn't above letting them bounce. It passed the day, at the least.

All these separate people in their cars or vans – or in the artic – shunted on towards the tunnel. The roadworks drew steadily nearer. The sun shone. The heat burned. All these people sat and sweated and itched and felt the irritations of the hold-up in their separate and different ways, vaguely sensing that this was a day bred for violence.

Separate, distinct, strangers – each car load – and yet they were bound together by the events of that hot and burning hold-up day.

Easing towards the intersection of the solid line of vehicles in the left-hand lane and the drivers attempting to fit in from the right, Bert Williams flicked on the left-turn indicator. The tick-ticking added another grasshopper note of madness to the scene. Alf Hardstaff rustled his paper and looked out the left-side window.

'Very nice!' he said in that tone of voice that instantly told Williams just what his mate was looking at.

Being a beefy, butch, virile cove, just like his mate, Williams craned to look.

The sports car rolling smoothly along in the inner lane was an Aston Martin V8 – enough to turn heads at the best

8

of times – but the driver took both men's attention. Luscious, shaped, just about decently clad for the weather, her blonde hair swirling half-confined by a motoring scarf, she smiled up at them and flicked her hand in a vague welcoming gesture.

'Very nice,' said Williams. 'But it's too hot for it.'

'It's never too hot,' said young Hardstaff, ogling. 'She's letting you in.'

The van driver lifted his hand in a thank you gesture and eased the wheel over to the left.

'Wish,' said Alf, 'she'd do the same for me.'

The two lanes of traffic narrowed down now as the two lines merged. Williams let rip a ripe chuckle, fat and contented.

'You never give up, do you, you randy sod? Anyway, she's out of your class.'

'Get away, Bert. No such thing as class these days. She'd lap it up – '

A chorus of car horns breaking like a wave from behind them halted Alf's words. The horns sounded off, bleeping and tootling. A dark green transit van sped at breakneck speed up the empty right-hand lane, hurtling along, raising a cloud of concrete dust. The transit van belted past.

'The lunatic,' shouted Williams, startled.

The transit sped past the cars tailing the security van. Each of these drivers linked together on this day reacted in their own special way, as human beings, fed-up with the delay, the stifling heat, the stink of fumes and the blare of radios.

Sumner said: 'What the – ' And sawed his precious Rover a trifle, wondering what he'd do to the maniac if he hit the caravan.

The transit roared past George Smiley who looked down from the cab of his artic with a look of utter contempt on his face. He'd seen it before. He'd seen the aftermath in fog – crumpled cars, smashed like aluminium foil, the dribbling blood across the hardtop, the sheeted bodies being carried

9

off. 'Another bloody maniac,' he said to himself.

Gerald Lewis, the car driver immediately abaft the security van, became aware of the chorus of honking horns as the transit abruptly appeared from his right-hand side. Lewis had got himself nicely positioned to take the gap between the Keep Left sign and the left-hand rail of the roadway. Now this unthinking, rude, incredibly oafish dolt was coming pushing and bustling in. For a moment Lewis was tempted to bang his right foot down on the throttle and surge ahead, forcing the van to back off; but he did not do so. He eased up. The security van drew ahead, close on the tail of a nondescript, seven-year-old Cortina held together by good luck, baling wire and, thought Lewis in his present savage mood, probably a forged MOT.

Lewis's car was still rolling forward. The transit braked fiercely and slewed, tyres smoking in the heat, swerved skidding across to come to a shuddering halt broadside on across the road. It effectively stopped all traffic. Lewis slammed on the brakes, jolting his wife and young Ronald forward. His wife's fat and the seat belt stopped her forward movement; in the rear young Ronald was thrown against the front seats, from where he slid to the floor, yelping in shock.

'Hey!' shouted Lewis. 'The fool! What's he up to?'

'He almost killed us!' Mrs Lewis's near-collapse had vanished, and her agitation became alarm. She twisted around. 'Jimmy!' She always called young Ronald Jimmy, to his fury. 'You all right, Jimmy?'

'Yes, Mum.'

The traffic was now snarled solid. Lewis started to open his door. 'What the devil does he think he's up to?'

'Leave it, Gerald – ' Mrs Lewis fancied she knew the outcome of this, and did not like it. It was too hot.

'Leave it? A headcase like that?' Lewis felt the relief that he hadn't tried to baulk the van off. If he had – the thought made him momentarily ill. The accident would have been bad enough; but his car! All the time and money he'd spent

10

making it smart, all the gadgets – yes, that was true. But he wanted a word with the fellow in the van. 'I won't leave it,' he said, ignoring his wife's repeated plea to forget it.

Lewis was tall and thin, with a sandy moustache. He wore an open-necked sports shirt and shared that style of dressing with millions of others. He was just a man, just a fed-up driver in a long, hot and stinking queue. He got out of the car and started to strut towards the transit.

The nondescript Cortina ahead of the security van stopped.

The traffic ahead of it moved on, dwindling away through the single-lane section, past the heaps of earth and the shovels, the yellow-painted excavators and a JCB, with the workmen trying to look as though they were busily putting right the road surface.

In that parcel of stalled cars the people were coming closer to their moment of togetherness. They looked out on to the brilliantly-lit scene. Some wiped the sweat away from their foreheads, others flicked a trickle of sweat away from the sides of their noses, others blinked their eyes in the glare. They all reacted in different ways, and yet, at the rock-bottom of their behaviour, they all felt exactly the same.

Sumner opened his car door and got out of his precious Rover 3500. Lewis was moving towards the broadside-on transit. Bilston, letting go Brenda's hand, climbed out of the Mini to see what the fuss was about.

The door of the beat-up Cortina opened quickly and a man dressed in levis and a windcheater got out quickly. He ran back towards the stopped security van. From the transit two more men got out. They carried shotguns.

All three men wore grotesque Hallowe'en masks.

The plastic masks convoluted in inane grins, the puffed cheeks shinily red, the eyebrows contorted.

The masks shone brightly in the strong sunlight.

Lewis saw the shotguns. He stopped. He froze. He felt ill.

The other people confronted by this moment of destiny – this moment when each one knew he could be killed, blown

11

apart, wasted – stopped, staring in disbelief.

They recognised what was going on. It was outside their personal experience; but now everything added up.

These three men wearing the grotesque Hallowe'en masks were raiders, armed with explosives and shotguns, and their target was the security van and the money or whatever it contained.

Frightened squeals broke from the Lewis's car. Mrs Lewis leaned out, shattered. 'Gerald!' she called; but her throat dried up and she couldn't go on.

Lewis stopped, frozen, unmoving, sweating.

Sumner stepped back to his Rover. He did not look at his car but stuck his hand in through the open window.

'Give me that camera!' he said, in the old Marines' way.

The two raiders with shotguns held them as though they knew what they were for and how to use them.

The man with the explosives kit moved swiftly to the rear of the security van. Lewis was looking directly into the figure-of-eight shape of the shotgun muzzles. The other raider let his shotgun circle the others in the nearest cars.

'Now,' said the raider. 'Don't be heroes – any of you.'

The explosives man taped a thick circle of cortex around the van's lock. It looked as though he had looped a coil of washing line around the lock. A pair of thin wires reeled out. The raider moved smartly away. Everyone – passengers and raiders alike – tensed. The raiders knew what was to happen. The frightened people in their cars or standing like dummies by the car doors could only guess, held in that fraught moment of feeling that destiny coalesced around them.

The cortex blew as the bell battery switch was made.

Perhaps the thought that this was a moment of destiny was too grand for a squalid occasion. A security van and a raid and shotguns and explosives – these things *did* belong on a concrete road in the bright sunshine, for they were part of life in the latter end of the twentieth century.

The cortex blew. The explosion stuttered up in the slot of blinding concrete, bellowing back in a wave of sound. Smoke billowed. A round hole matching the loop of cortex appeared blackly in the rear door of the security van.

The explosion brought Bert Williams out of his van. He saw the smoke, saw the still figures of people grouped oddly.

'I don't believe it!' he said, stepping out on to the road.

'What?' demanded Alf Hardstaff, unable to see from his position.

The two shotguns menaced the passengers in and out of their cars. The people stood as though petrified into mere columns of concrete sprouting from the baking concrete all about.

The third raider ripped open the rear doors of the van.

Everyone, petrified or not, could see the security guard, see his panic-stricken white face under the big shiny helmet with the black chin strap. He crouched in the rear opening, his hands half-raised, looking out, blinking in the abrupt glare.

The first raider swung back from the crowd. He put the shotgun into his right shoulder. He bent – only a little, only a little, for the range was dreadfully short. He fired both barrels. Bang – bang.

The security guard vanished backwards.

He was not a pretty sight – what was left.

He flopped back into the shadows of the van's interior. Terence Lansbury was out of his Avenger. He did not quite know what he felt. With a quick word of reassurance to his two Labradors, he hurried along the line of stalled cars. He couldn't understand himself. He called to the other drivers and passengers.

'Did you *see* that, all of you?'

Jack and Brenda Bilston heard him. Bilston turned back to the Mini and fished out the stills camera – a medium-priced little thing but, he felt, perfectly adequate for this – and he clicked off a shot of the security van, the open doors, the raiders with their shotguns. A little smoke still hung in the stifling air. The tang of burnt powder tangled and bit with the cortex smoke, rubber and concrete dust and exhaust smoke; the cutting resembled a cocktail of aromas.

Lansbury hurried on. Sweat trickled into his eyes and he blinked. Suppose these men shot his dogs? No – he reached the raider and, blindly, clawed at him – no, no, he couldn't let that happen.

Lansbury was elderly and didn't know it; he tried to do something and the raider simply brushed him off, bellowing an obscenity. Frantically, Lansbury grabbed at the man and the grotesque Hallowe'en mask caught in his fingers. He pulled. The mask slid sideways on its elastic band. Part of the man's face showed, a gaunt jaw, unshaven, a hollow cheek and prominent cheek bone. The man yelled again and brought the shotgun butt down on Lansbury's head. The elderly estate car driver collapsed. Lansbury pitched forward on to his knees on the concrete. He hung for a moment, as though in prayer, swaying. Then he fell to sprawl on his face, tearing his cheek on the harshly-ribbed concrete.

The girl in the Aston-Martin V8 screamed, screamed, shrieking: 'Help him! Someone – help that old man!'

The van driver and his mate jumped down. They didn't believe what they were seeing and hearing and smelling. But it was happening. Bert Williams and Alf Hardstaff began to run up the line of cars.

In the background a monstrous yellow shape loomed.

The three raiders began to back off, two shotguns held ready to shoot, the reloading – Sumner recognised proficiency when he saw it – done with speed and despatch.

'We said no heroes!' the first raider called. His body tensed, rigid in the sunlight. The shotgun swung with freezing menace, chilling sweat cold, running a trickle of ice down sweat-heated bodies. 'Stay away!'

George Smiley saw a chance and slammed the big artic into gear. He swung the articulated cab across the road, right-handed. The massive body blocked off the road. The raiders' transit could not now return along the right-hand lane and it could not go ahead because of the roadworks. George Smiley felt he had contributed something. He jumped from the cab, feeling more lively than he had for years.

A powerful engine note from up ahead brought the raiders' attention from the artic blocking their escape down the cutting. The JCB was rolling down towards the clapped-out Cortina. The JCB looked immense. Painted a vivid yellow, almost brand-new, it rolled ponderously and with enormous panache along the concrete. Lefty Plant, wrestling the controls, handled the monster perfectly. He'd hoisted up the rear hoe on its universal arms, swinging it out of the way. The front bucket was lowered to within six inches of the concrete. The massive rear wheels revolved so slowly that you could see the tread pattern like crevices, turning over, each revolution visibly urging the JCB on. Lefty handled her beautifully. He aimed the front bucket at the Cortina.

Lefty sat at his controls in the high-sided, square, glassed-in box that served as a driving cab. He felt like God. The bucket caught at the Cortina. Lefty hit with just the right speed, and the bucket lifted just right. The Cortina lurched and rolled over with a great rending of metal that made Lefty's day.

A raider swung his shotgun up and let fly.

Lefty just had time to get his head down before the front of the cab exploded into a sharding whirring mass of glass.

The raiders stared about, backing off. Their Cortina was an overturned wreck. The transit was blocked off by the artic. The van driver and his mate and the lorry driver moved in. The Mini driver followed them, stopping every now and then to shoot another picture. Gerald Lewis saw it all, standing stiff and rigid.

Young Ronald jumped up and down, almost incoherent with excitement. 'Go on, Dad!' screamed young Ronald.

Gerald Lewis just stood. The other people were moving on, following the raiders as they backed off. A kind of animal stealth informed the people's movements; the raiders backed and the people followed them as though drawn by invisible chains.

But Lewis just stood. He was petrified – but not petrified enough to miss the feeling in his guts. He did not know what to call that sick, stomach-upsetting, dizzy and disgusting feeling – certainly fear was not nearly a strong enough word – but whatever it might be called in the medical dictionary he knew what it was doing. He could not move. He couldn't have moved if they'd shot his wife's head off and blown a hole through young Ronald.

The whining note of a racing police car reached the people moving in their drama in the concrete slot. The siren ululated up from the back of the queue, rapidly drawing nearer.

The raiders backed off. They ran across to the embankment of the cutting and began to climb up.

Bert and Alf bent near the roadworks and picked up chunks of rock, brickbats. The panda car slid up in a cloud of dust and a very young police constable jumped out. His face shone.

He looked up.

The raiders were almost at the overpass bridge. The iron railings cut sharp rectangles against the light. Sumner tilted his cine camera up to take it all in. He felt pleased that he had, with the little extra commission money, decided to buy a power-driven and not a hand-wound model. The police constable started around his car and the lowest raider let fly with his shotgun. The blast took out the panda car's windscreen The constable ducked down. The van men were hurling lumps of rock, they ducked back, too. Bert Williams hefted two half bricks, one in each hand.

The constable looked across, taking it all in, looking again upslope to where the raiders were climbing over the railings. He could just see the top of a car there – looked like a Jaguar.

Bert Williams banged the two half-bricks together. He spoke viciously. 'I'd like to give 'em all a wax job!'

The three bandits vanished over the railings on to the overpass road. The Jaguar started up and slid away, burning rubber, belting off and away into the sunshine.

The people were left in that stinking, burning, hellish concrete slot. Cars and vans snarled across the road, the gaping earth of the roadworks, the towering yellow shapes of the earthmoving equipment, added a fantastic note. Lefty Plant shook his head. The foreman came up, red-faced, not quite knowing what to shout.

'That was a nice thirty-pence-worth,' said Lefty.

'What?' The foreman looked even more shattered.

'It costs six pounds an hour to hire a JCB with driver – this little lot cost you thirty pence, I reckon,' said Lefty Plant. 'If you don't count it as overtime.'

Chapter Two

Sumner's film was processed so rapidly once the police were aware of its existence that a print could be delivered into the anonymous building just off Whitehall in record time. In the shabby interior of the building, where only the communications and electronics sections, the forensic laboratory and one or two other areas of ultra-modern efficiency showed up the rest of the place, the discreet signs directed people to shadowy departments. This was the headquarters of C.I.5, Criminal Intelligence Five.

In the chief's darkened office, Sumner's film was run for the edification of Cowley's top agents. The men sat quietly, watching as the film picked up the security van raid, the shotguns, the blast that killed the guard, the actions of the artic and the JCB, the escape of the raiders, the panda car's arrival.

'Good for old Joe Public,' said Doyle, watching the film.

'Yes.' Cowley sat contained within himself, stocky, rugged, the absolute boss of this organisation, a man dedicated to crime prevention. Serving as an administrator in M.I.5 he had at first been resented for his bluff ways, ultimately he had become the most respected of administrators. He had been handed the assignment by the Home Secretary and the Home Office with the full concurrence of Service and Police Chiefs of turning his unrivalled expertise in the field of military intelligence against domestic crime. He had taken up the task with enthusiasm. C.I.5 – the Action Squad, the Big A – had powers to investigate in any area in the furtherance of their duty.

The methods of the Big A were unconventional. Very unconventional. As Cowley would say – fight fire with fire.

The agents with him now watching the film were men who shared his ideology. They wanted results in the fight against crime and they got results. How they got those results was their business.

The men in C.I.5 were special. Handpicked from those walks of life where men learned to handle themselves, to be tough and yet know how to use that toughness – men from S.A.S., from the Marines, from the Police forces of the country, they were men who carried a special responsibility.

Men like Bodie and Doyle. As the film wound through to the end and the Jaguar sped away, the murky film shaking with the trembling of Sumner's hands, Cowley regarded Doyle and Bodie.

Ray Doyle, nearly thirty, finest shot with a handgun in the entire Met, detective constable before he'd joined C.I.5, Doyle might be inclined towards being a dreamer – he'd taken art classes and always firmly denied he'd ever drooled over the nudes – but he knew his job nowadays. Born in South London, he'd come up the hard way. And, with all this, there was a touch of morality about Ray Doyle that perhaps marked him off from the other hard men of the Big A. Cowley, as far as ever he would, reposed complete trust in Doyle. Tommy McKay, now Shotgun Tommy, was a different proposition entirely. Cowley worried about Shotgun Tommy. And Dick Mason – morality for Mason meant getting the job done with the least inconvenience to innocent bystanders, which was a standing tenet of C.I.5.

And Bodie. William Andrew Philip Bodie. That was his name; but Bodie would answer to Bodie and nothing else. He was a couple of years younger than Doyle, his partner; but you'd easily take him for older. As for his background – the more he romanced about it the more it grew luridly. He had joined the Merchant Navy when he was seventeen, jumped ship and joined a mercenary force in Africa, lived with – and off – an older woman in Cape Town, joined the Colours

19

when he was twenty-three and made it to sergeant in the Parachute Regiment. To look at Bodie, the dark one, you'd take him for a star striker, playing for a top club, capped for England, a terror in front of the net, knocking 'em in.

Doyle was the fair one, with a cap of tousled curls, round faced, relaxed. Bodie was the dark, intense one, who could handle himself, and knew it, and knew how to contain his aggressions – well, most of the time.

As the film of the security van raid wound down Bodie stretched. 'The security guard?'

'Killed outright.' Cowley still regarded these men as the lights in his shabby office went on.

'According to the Press,' said Doyle. 'It was a bullion raid gone wrong. Silver.'

'That's right,' nodded Cowley. 'According to the Press.'

Bodie and Doyle knew George Cowley. They sensed something – and God knew what – was coming.

'So,' said Doyle, carefully casual. 'Why the picture show?' When Cowley said nothing, Doyle went on: 'Why should we be interested in a bullion raid that went wrong?'

Without conscious theatricality, and yet fully aware of the way it would sound, Cowley said: 'Because it wasn't exactly a bullion raid.' He paused, and in his voice with that distant Northern burr, finished: 'And it didn't exactly go wrong.'

Doyle harked back to his original comment. 'But those people – they risked their lives – having a go –' Police officers – and Doyle could not forget his years with the Force held ambivalent feelings about Joe Q. Public having a go.

'Look and listen,' said Cowley. He moved to the video machine wired to the TV and switched it on at a predetermined selection. The screen lit up and a recording of a newscast filled the room with sound and colour.

There was the concrete slot, with traffic passing smoothly through the single-lane past the roadworks. There were the overpasses above. But on the screen the stink of it, the feel of the heat, the taste of diesel fumes and concrete dust on lips and tongue were all absent. Fronting the camera a well-known news-reporter read his lines from the idiot board with the panache of an old pro.

'. . . on the approach road this afternoon,' he was saying at the point Cowley clued in, ' . . . when a guard was killed. Silver bullion, worth approximately a quarter of a million pounds, was left untouched as the killers made good their escape . . . '

Cowley broke in, speaking with a heaviness that caused further premonitions to Bodie and Doyle, who wanted the chief to get to the nitty gritty. 'See how easy,' said Cowley. 'How easy it is to fool the people, tell 'em lies?'

The news reporter went on: 'The raid was foiled by members of the public who bravely . . . '

Cowley punched the stop key. He looked up, his face with its lines and creases of good humour wrinkled into a bitterness that he did not often show. Cowley was feeling this one.

'Even that poor fool doesn't know.'

Bodie looked at Doyle. He it was who said, for both of them: 'And what about these poor fools?'

Cowley stared at him. He shook his head. Then, slowly, he said: 'Ever heard the name John Gerry Patterson?'

Bodie said: 'No.'

Doyle said: 'Yes.'

Cowley cocked an eye at him.

'Some loud-mouthed American politician.'

Cowley nodded. 'Loud-mouthed, rich, stupid. A hell-raiser. A fire-brand. "Senator in one year, President in three" was just one of his well-worn phrases. A clown. A people's clown.'

'But,' said Brodie. 'A very important clown?'

'Oh, yes. And, last week, against all protests, this very important people's clown decided to visit the place of his ancestors – decided to visit this country.' Cowley stared at them. 'John Gerry Patterson and the people. That was another of his favourite sayings.'

'I didn't know he was here,' offered Doyle, expecting the come-back that Cowley would certainly provide.

'Neither did I. So why should you? Only a handful of people did know. A few Government officials, and the men who did the hit.' At this Bodie and Doyle saw it, and waited while Cowley filled in the details. 'There was an assassination threat, here on our soil. A straight threat. A heavy threat. A promise threat. Made by the kind of jokers who would blow an airliner out of the sky for a good cause and an even better pay-day.'

Doyle shook his head, already beginning to wonder who had fouled up so monumentally. 'So we had to get him out fast, under cover, in a security van that was pretending to be carrying silver bullion.'

'Only instead it was carrying dear old John Gerry Patterson dressed as a guard.' Bodie knew. 'That's it?'

'That,' said George Cowley with heavy sourness, bitterness, resentment, 'Is it.'

Tactfully, the partners said nothing whilst Cowley turned back to the video machine and thumbed it on again. The sunglare in the concrete slot seemed to bring waves of visible heat into the room, and with them the stifling air, the smell of exhausts and hot rubber. The TV reporter had grouped a number of the people who had taken part in the day's drama. They stood in a little group facing the camera, shuffling, looking shy or nervous or uncomfortable – each according to his ways as a human being. Distinct, separate, but on this day they were all bell-tolling John Donne's, chained into a circumstance that held them fast locked together.

Bert Williams, the van driver, spoke up, haltingly.

' . . . Well, you don't think, I mean, at the time, do you? But, well, you have to have a go. Sort of – seemed right. The right thing to do.'

Watching him and the other people there, people he had seen in the shaky, blurry amateur cine film, Cowley felt the bile rising in his throat.

The van driver went on; and Cowley saw the shy pride

22

there, and writhed. 'And I suppose,' said the van driver. 'Thanks to us, they didn't succeed.'

Cowley slammed the video machine off.

'John Gerry Patterson *and* the people.'

'And the killers, whoever they are, are long gone.' Doyle was already wondering, as previously, how C.I.5 fitted in. George Cowley wouldn't mess in a dead case, unless facts brought the case alive again.

'No,' said Cowley. Bodie and Doyle looked fixedly at him. Now, they were thinking, we get to it. 'I'm only guessing; but I think so. Every airport and exit was sewn up tight within five minutes of the attack. And I mean sewn up. Tighter than a Scot on Burns Night. I'm betting – I'm *gambling* – they're still here – somewhere.'

As Doyle said: 'Okay. So they'll lie low, go to earth,' so Cowley manipulated the machine and threw up on to the screen that picture of the raider with his grotesque Hallowe'en mask half twisted aside.

'A clear ID.'

Bodie snorted. 'Come on, sir! That could be anybody!'

'*They* don't know that.' Some of the bitterness leached away from Cowley. He spoke in that plummy voice with a trace of smugness. 'The Press are hungry for a story. I've given them one. We have a clear ID on film.'

'And plenty of eye-witnesses to back it up,' said Doyle. He saw the angles. This could prove the cheese for the trap.

A discreet tap at the door heralded the arrival of the chief's secretary, Betty. Both Doyle and Bodie turned to enjoy the sight of a luscious female, with a wiggle that could raise a head of steam on an iceberg, with a figure that – and eyes that – and that – all wrapped up in that same damned iceberg. Bodie still wasn't sure if Doyle had spoken the truth, and Doyle still harboured deep suspicions about Bodie where the fabulous Betty was concerned. Both partners could pull birds with a consummate ease they exercised as a God-given privilege. But with Betty the privilege always seemed to expire into a frozen smile of such sweetness it could have blown

23

the best safe in the deepest vaults of the tightest bank in London.

Now Betty laid the afternoon papers down on Cowley's desk, smiled at them, whereat they smiled back, like clowns, and departed. Any other girl, *any* other girl, they both said to themselves, and . . .

Cowley's voice reached them. He looked stricken. He held the top paper up as though it had been found clogging a lavatory on Paddington Station.

'The Press release,' he said in a strangled voice. 'Don't they realise what they're doing? Don't they realise what they've done!'

Bodie and Doyle whipped the other paper up and scanned the black headlines, saw the story, there in black and white.

'Who gave them permission?' Cowley started to yell. 'My God! The imbeciles! They've published the names and addresses of the witnesses! For God's sake!'

Chapter Three

The derelict warehouse due for demolition hung creakingly
from ancient, grimy Victorian brickwork. The arches sagged.
The floors were death traps, the ceilings fallen away. Dust
and cobwebs shrouded the cavernous floors with a miasmic
gloom. The distant sounds of the docks floated in, and the
smell of long-gone commerce hung about the encrusted walls.

Tin Can finished up cleaning up the area used by the four
white men who had paid him plentifully in the kind of pay
Tin Can would do anything for. He picked up the three grotesque facemasks, and he thought of the old times, back in
Trinidad, and he did not sigh; for those days were dead.

A tall, thin, gangling man, Tin Can, hooked on the stuff
and knowing he would die from it one day – but, until then,
with a pusher he could always hit for a sack or two, he'd
enjoy life while he could. He went around the forlorn area
cleaning up after the four white men.

The three of them here now sat grumpily on old crates, a
petrol tin, lackadaisically playing cards, although the cards
could never hold their full attention until the job was
finished.

They had discarded the face masks. The damn things
itched and sweated in the heat, and the three who had done
the work down in the cutting were scathing about the fourth
raider's golden-balls in having the cushy job of just driving
the Jag away.

Charley glanced across at Tin Can. He could still remember the way that old fool had clawed at his mask.

'What are we going to do about him when we leave? He's *seen* us. He's loose in the head.'

Bert chucked a king of spades down and said with meaning: 'Even looser in the mouth.'

'That's what I mean. What are we going to do about him?'

'He,' said Georgey, continuing to play cards, 'will die of natural causes.'

'You can guarantee that?'

'Yes, I can guarantee that.' Georgey pulled a package out of his pocket and placed it neatly on the table among the cards. 'He's got a bad habit. And there's enough stuff in there to send him out of his skull – and, then, to the morgue.'

The three men chuckled at this, satisfied, and then looked up as Karl entered carrying an evening paper. These men, whilst they were all different one from another as to faces and speech and mannerisms, held contained within themselves like tightly coiled springs the same intense hardness, viciousness, the same intemperance. These men were professionals who would kill to avoid being taken up. They were dangerous.

Tin Can whistled as he shuffled about cleaning up the mess of empty tins and abandoned plastic cartons, the crumpled cans of beer, the cigarette packets.

'Read this!' said Karl, slapping the evening paper down over the cards and the ominous, deadly, white packet.

'One positive identification, a man is now being sought.' Georgey looked up from the black lines of print. 'That's you, Charley.'

'That mask wasn't off for more than a few seconds! That silly old bastard – I should have killed him. I knew I should have killed him.' He looked most upset. 'Means I can't go home today. Have to lie low.'

'We'll *all* have to lie low.'

'Evidence on film doesn't hold up in court,' said Bert, picking his teeth reflectively. 'I read that somewhere. Some judges won't even allow it.'

'They will,' snarled Georgey, 'when it's backed by an eye-witness!'

However run-down in appearance the anonymous building off Whitehall might be, the operations room and the associated electronics and communications section was, in the words of daily papers who knew nothing about what went on in C.I.5, ultra-modern. Cowley had only to push buttons to be in instant communication with his agents. Now, furious, seething with a rage that was as much inwardly directed as anywhere, he detailed off his men. Bodie and Doyle. McKay and Wilson. Mason and Crabtree. Bain and Wesley. Biggs, Lofthouse, Jones, Thomas.

'Bodyguard job,' said Cowley in the voice that brought his men's senses quivering up, alert, immediately responsive. 'The full works for a dozen witnesses. Mr and Mrs Bilston, newly weds on honeymoon somewhere in Surrey. Gerald Lewis – '

He listened for a space and then, with a quiet cutting viciousness said: 'If I knew where the lovenest was in Surrey I would tell you! Find it, before the yobs do. George Smiley, truck driver, now working for the LMN Company . . . '

He detailed the assignments. Those stupid damn papers!

At the trucking company with the loud LMN sign painted up over the main gate the drivers went about their usual routine. They were aware of what old George had been up to, and marvelled, although those who claimed to know him best said that was just like old George Smiley.

A beat-up Cortina eased into the yard. The driver looked as battered as the car, scruffy, denimed, with a lean nasty look to his jaws, a fey light in his pale eyes. He leaned over the back seat and flicked a dirty raincoat over the shotgun on the back seat. Then he picked up the raincoat-swathed gun and got out. He didn't bother to lock the door.

The shotgun was a twelve-bore, a pump-action job, with the barrel cut down to nearly the end of the slide action. It was a Remington Model 870 Magnum. In the hands of a shooter who knew how to use it, loaded with five big three-inch Magnum shells, it could devastate a regiment of charging berserkers.

Enquiries elicited the fact that George Smiley hadn't come back yet. He'd probably, the mechanic said, wiping his hands on an oily scrap of cotton waste, dropped off at the Ace Café.

'Popular today, our George,' said the mechanic. 'Some other fellers asking about him, five, ten minutes ago – '

The mechanic blinked. The scruffy-looking character with the oddly-rolled raincoat was leaping like a maniac back into his car, tooling the cropped-off Cortina out of the gate in a swirling cloud of dust, burning rubber along the road to the Ace Café.

George Smiley patted his stomach as he left the Ace Café and started towards his lorry. Alice's tea and buns always went down a treat. He'd passed a few words with the drivers there, muted, down-beat, talking about the raid in the tunnel approach cutting.

A black Jaguar parked close alongside Smiley's big LMN truck. The Jag, although dusty and not in its first immaculate condition, still managed to look a little odd among the lorries and trucks. Smiley headed past the Jaguar towards his cab, and the Jaguar driver's voice halted him.

'George Smiley?'

Half-turning, already beginning to smile at the thought that here came another question about the hold-up, Smiley looked at the Jaguar. He saw the driver looking up and then a movement in the passenger window caught his attention.

George Smiley looked back – and saw the last thing he ever saw on this earth.

The barrels of the shotgun poked out of the window. Both barrels went off. Smiley was picked up and hurled backwards against his own truck. His blood blew out in a red fountain. His body hit the aluminium panelled truck. For an instant he hung there, shot through, hanging crucified against the aluminium. Then he fell. Blood streaked in huge blobs down the metal.

George Smiley hit the dusty ground of the Ace Café's car park and sprawled, face down, spread-out, motionless.

The black Jaguar started up and sped for the gate.

An old beat-up Cortina driving madly in, almost collided with the Jag. The two cars swerved, rocking on their springs. Then the Jaguar sped away. The Cortina driver saw Smiley's corpse by the truck, saw the obscene trails of blood down the aluminium. The Cortina did not stop. It swirled around, tyres screeching, scything up a cloud of dust, belted back out of the gate after the Jaguar.

The Cortina driver looked ahead to where the Jaguar was speeding down between the backs of warehouses, the over-head lines swooping up and down with the speed of move-ment to the eyes, pedestrians leaping out of the way. He flicked a switch and a siren started up, howling away as the Cortina sped in chase.

The car was a rusty beat-up wreck; but it travelled fast on new tyres. The driver unhooked a shiny radio-handset from under the battered dash. The handset looked incongruous in that near-wreck of a car.

He said: 'McKay to H.Q.'

Instantly George Cowley's voice crackled up from the speaker.

'Tommy? Come in.'

'Found the driver, Smiley, at the Ace Café.'

'Good. All quiet, is it?'

'It will be when I catch up with them.'

Cowley's voice said: 'Catch up with who?'

'I don't,' said Tommy McKay, 'know until I catch up with them, do I? The guys who wasted the truck driver, George Smiley.'

'What!' Cowley's voice blasted from the speaker. Tommy McKay could visualise only too clearly how the chief was reacting. Tommy didn't think too much about that. He gave

29

his location and direction and, just before he snapped the off switch, said: 'I'll be in touch.'

The Cortina swirled along after the black Jaguar, sending people diving to safety on corners, hurdling intersections and avoiding cross-traffic. Shotgun Tommy was out after prey.

George Cowley contacted Bodie and Doyle on the radio net and bellowed at them to get after Tommy McKay – fast. 'Find him,' said Cowley. 'Help him. And report.'

Bodie frowned. 'Find him – help him –'

Doyle said viciously: 'He means stop him.'

'Yes – before it develops into a massacre.'

When they screeched to a halt by Tommy's old Cortina in the run-down warehouse area and jumped out, the sounds of gunfire blasted from the ground floor. Moving with the stealthy and yet rapid motion of hunters they hit the warehouse, slid in through the door, and then froze. The darkness intershot with random streaks of light made the interior fuzzy – and dangerous.

'Be cool with Tommy, Bodie. You know he's crazy.'

'Cowley wouldn't accept that. Nobody in C.I.5 is crazy.'

'Motivated, then.' They spoke in whispers, their eyes searching the area, their guns in their fists, lethal hunters, yet perfectly able to carry on a bantering conversation as they stalked killers. No – nobody in C.I.5 was crazy – but it helped to be a little loose in the head, all the same, at certain times.

'His whole family was wiped out by terrorists.'

'Unlucky,' said Bodie, cryptically. He slid behind a splintered crate, the Browning Hi-Power in his fist cocked up. 'That they overlooked Tommy.'

'That,' said Doyle, passionately, 'is a lousy thing to say.'

'Tommy's a lousy thing to be. He's kill crazy.'

Ahead of them a more solid wall bulked, shadowed, beckoning.

Doyle looked at Brodie. 'And what makes you so different?'

Bodie regarded his partner for a moment. Then, quietly, he said: 'The difference is – I do it – but I don't enjoy it.'

They moved on and before Doyle could come back they saw Tommy McKay leaning against the wall, cradling the sawn-off. He saw them and his face went mean. 'Cowley!' he said in a disgusted tone.

'No, Tommy, it's just a coincidence.' Bodie smiled. 'Short cut to the supermarket.'

'Short cut to hell unless you keep your head down.'

Bodie and Doyle moved against the wall. 'How many?'

'Three, at the least. Three handguns and a sawn-off and whatever else they have stashed away in there.' Tommy put a finger through the bullet hole in his old blue jean coat.

The space between them and where the gunmen were holed up gaped ominously, leering at them, taunting, shadowed.

'No Man's land,' said Bodie.

Tommy let a little chuckle dribble out. 'Somebody has to cross it.' He pushed away from the wall. 'If we're going to be home in time for tea.'

Bodie and Doyle saw Tommy walk, upright and stiff, out across that open space. The grimy concrete absorbed the sound of his footfalls. The partners breathed shallowly. Shotgun Tommy might not be crazy; but he was so close to that vague line as to make little difference. Bodie and Doyle recognised a man who had suffered too much, and now didn't care what happened just so the suffering would stop – didn't care if he did get killed. Might welcome it. A man of violence, welcoming the terminal violence that would end all the suffering for him.

So, because in all the stupid tangle of emotions, and pride, and loyalty, and courage, and things that could get a man killed, they had to do it. Bodie and Doyle rose. They walked out on to that open space among the shadows and the bars of light. The three men walked forward together.

Bodie, it was, who said: 'Can I ask just one question?'

Eyes fixed ahead, shotgun at the ready, Tommy said: 'Yeh.'

'Why are we walking?'

'It's a lot of space.' The feyness in Tommy prickled at

31

Bodie. 'Run or walk. It'll make no difference.'

They were exposed, naked, walking forward across that space of grimy concrete towards the waiting guns.

'Only,' said Bodie, and the conversational tone of his voice matched perfectly the way he spoke. 'No one's given me a choice.'

'Then make a choice.'

They walked on. Bodie looked at the menacing shadows. 'Thanks.'

He took off sprinting fast. He slammed head on for the shadows and the waiting guns.

Before he had taken three strides Doyle was belting along at his side.

Four strides and Tommy took off, also. Better to get there alive than shot through full of holes. What happened after that wouldn't then matter so much.

The stairs loomed above them, cobwebby, enticing them to death.

Using their skills, both the unconscious reflexes learned by their ancestors fighting tooth and claw to survive, and the sophisticated combat techniques taught at secret and not-so-secret military academies, they combed the warehouse, going up the stairs, checking each floor. Nothing. Empty. Deserted. Only dust and cobwebs and shadows.

Then they reached the top floor.

A tousled pile of blankets ruffled into a corner alerted them. A couple of cigarette butts tossed down and ground flat told them that if the birds had flown this was the nest. A large box stood to one side with a cigarette carton, ripped open, caught and hanging down one side. Somebody had been trying to clean the place up. A noise broke hollow, scraping and muffled, from a side door.

Without having to signal their intentions, the agents positioned themselves. Bodie to one side, Doyle the other. Tommy stood with the pump-action shotgun thrust out from his hip, leg half-bent, standing like some pop star with a guitar, a guitar designed to kill with shotgun shells and not with sound. Bodie reached for the door, seized the knob, jerked it open.

A weird figure lurched out.

A tall, skinny, loose-limbed figure broke from the door. Its high-peaked shoulders shook, not so much to the sound of unheard music as to some enormous private joke. The figure wore tattered jeans and a checked shirt with a once-zippy waistcoat.

But the thing that held and gripped the three C.I.5 men was the grotesque mask over the man's face. The Hallowe'en mask caught the random shaft of light from a splintered gap in the roof and its bright plastic colouring shone out brilliantly. The agents knew where they had seen a mask like that before, where they had seen three masks like that – the filmed record made by Sumner rose up pungently before them.

Tommy almost blasted the figure's guts out where it danced and capered, snapping its fingers, its long apparently boneless legs writhing like the tentacles of an octopus. Bodie was ready to snap off a couple of shots.

Ray Doyle jumped forward.

'No!' he bellowed.

Bodie was ready to follow his partner's lead; but Shotgun Tommy swivelled the muzzle, ready to pull the trigger. Bodie looked into the inner room, came back to report it empty. Doyle was staring at the weird masked figure.

'Tin Can?'

The lanky figure stayed plastered against the wall, shaking, jiggling, taking no notice of the men or of Tommy's shotgun.

'I know you,' said Doyle. He spoke to the other two C.I.5 men. 'He couldn't kill anyone. Only himself. And he's been doing that slowly for years. I busted him enough times when I was with Drugs.'

With a little apathetic struggle the mask was torn away.

Bodie said: 'Stoned out of his skull.'

Tin Can continued to weave and gyrate, completely oblivious of the men. Doyle tried to get through to him, guessing the Trinidadian had been looking after the raiders, anxious

3

to get the questions over with. After verbal prodding, Tin Can came back to the dull reality of the warehouse out of the glittering brilliance of the world in his own skull. He nodded, chuckling now, pleased with himself.

'They feed your head, Tin Can?'

'But not me belly. They fed me pockets.' Tin Can dug down into the back pocket as though suddenly remembering. He brought out a handful of crumpled fivers. 'See? Good pay day. They's good raj.'

Doyle moved closer. 'How many of 'em?'

'Card school.'

Doyle nodded. 'Four. Where are they now?'

'I dunno.'

'Where did they come from?'

'Everywhere.' He laughed again at his private joke. 'They come from everywhere. They's too smart for you, sunu.'

With the patience he had long cultivated as a detective constable handling childish people like this, Doyle asked what nationality they were.

'White,' said Tin Can.

'So how did they speak?'

'White.'

'Where have they gone, Tin Can?'

This was like a question and answer session in a dream-world.

'I dunno.' Tin Can began to gyrate again, his knees rubber, his arms weaving. 'I dunno. One minute they're finished. They's ready to split and run. Next minute they's staying. They has things to do.' Tin Can shook those peaked-up shoulders, swaying to the music and the joke in his skull. 'Important things.'

Bodie picked up the discarded newspaper.

'Yeah.' Bodie's face held that intense, downdrawn look of furious suppressed passion. 'A dozen important things. A dozen witnesses!'

Chapter Four

The Fox Inn boasted a superb cuisine and the best table wines, with the most comfortable beds for miles around. Deep in the heart of the Surrey countryside the hotel provided unobtrusive service of the finest. Jack and Brenda Bilston had made full use of the finest bed for miles, and had obtained some mileage from it themselves. Now a little fresh air was in order. So they strolled out into the grounds, heading for the bridge over the little stream. In the brilliant sunshine the sight and sound of running water would refresh them both.

They reached the rustic bridge, and heard the water chuckling by below, the gentle susurration of the trees. Quite unaffectedly they turned, on a single impulse, to kiss each other.

They did not see the car moving quietly along the gravelled side road. Had they seen it they would probably have gone on kissing each other. The kiss was far more important to them than anything else in the whole wide world – they would have thought.

And been wrong.

Or, on second thoughts, seeing the circumstances, be right – too dreadfully right.

Dick Mason and Tully Crabtree checked with the hotel receptionist who told them that Mr and Mrs Bilston had just gone out. The two C.I.5 men hurried from the hotel and headed across the grounds towards the stream.

Brenda could feel Jack's arm about her, and trembled with the sheer joy of living. She felt her new husband abruptly jerk in her arms, as though stung by a sudden shock. She had heard nothing. But Jack was slipping away, was falling through her arms. On his face the most dreadful expression twisted his lips – and –

And on his white shirt a red stain spread.

She saw the red stain and the small black hole at its centre. Jack toppled. He twisted over the rustic handrail. He fell into the stream.

She screamed.

Brenda Bilston screamed.

Mason and Crabtree running full tilt across the grass heard the scream. They whipped out their handguns and fired into the air, unable to see what the danger was. The warning shots had an effect. The cruising car abruptly accelerated away, and the last quick snap shots missed Mrs Brenda Bilston.

As the Big A men reached her she sank half-fainting to the bridge. They supported her. Her horrified eyes were glaring with a maniacal look at the body of her late husband, floating for a few moments face down in the water.

Perhaps, in her frame of mind at that dreadful moment, Brenda Bilston, widow, regretted that the gangsters' parting shots had missed her.

It was only when she became aware of the numbness in her shoulder that she realised they had not missed. But she was not dead. She was still alive and Jack was dead.

There did not seem any sense at all in the world to Brenda Bilston, then, no sense at all.

In Cowley's Spartan office he sat hunched, staring bleakly at the screen as he punched up the pictures of the witnesses. One by one the little video machine threw up the faces of these people, ordinary members of the public, who had thought to have a go and foil a 'daring bullion robbery'. The truck driver, George Smiley, was already dead. Now, as Bodie and Doyle entered, Cowley was trying to come to terms with the fresh deaths.

36

His powerful fingers gripped on to his bad leg. A bullet lodged there, a memento of a strafing Condor Legionary, gave him hell from time to time. Now was one of those times.

'I heard,' said Cowley. 'They're dead – aren't' they?'

'The girl's all right, sir. Shoulder wound. But she's okay.'

Bodie waited for his partner to finish. He was well aware of the powder-keg mood of the chief; but he had to say: 'Apart from that the honeymoon was fine.'

Doyle flashed a warning glare at Bodie; but Cowley snapped the video machine off and jerked around, clutching his leg. 'No, Doyle. Let him have his sick joke. Jokes are in order. Because the joke is on me. *I* killed them.'

'No,' said Doyle, positively, angry. 'The papers did that.'

'I should have anticipated that. If I'm worth anything in this job, it is because I have experience. I am *supposed* to have experience.' He cut a hand through the air. 'The Press did their job. While I wasn't doing mine.' The partners understood the anguish, and understood, too, how foolish it would be even to attempt to argue with Cowley. The chief snapped out: 'Tin Can?'

'Maybe, when they pump the junk out of him. He is one high man.' Doyle shook his head. 'And been dumped so many times his head has taken a beating. But he's our only link.'

'Exactly. He worked with these men.' Cowley cocked his fierce stare up at Doyle. 'He must know something – anything. Doyle?'

'I'll handle it.' Doyle took himself off.

Cowley nodded. 'Good.' He looked at the dark TV screen. 'Bodie – if another witness should die ...'

'We have our best boys playing nursemaid now. But I thought I might take a look – why don't you come along?' Bodie kept his voice firm, although immediately aware that Cowley had sussed him out, seen through his ploy to get the chief out of this dark mood. 'Might cheer them up. You too.'

'The day I cheer my men up,' Cowley told Bodie with a flash of the old spirit, 'I'll *know* I'm ready for the scrap heap.'

'For morale, then. And on the way – who knows? I might buy you a pure Malt Scotch.'

Cowley rose to his feet. Both he and Bodie knew the scheme had succeeded. 'You,' said Cowley, heading for the door. 'You're darned right you will.'

Bodie checked over the arrangements for Gerald Lewis. With gunmen able to move freely about – for the time being, at the least – they could choose their target. Cowley and Bodie eased up in the nearly deserted suburban street, turning the car into a side road long before the Lewis house. The lamps burned mellowly in their ranked rows, shrubberies carried that well-tended suburban look, the pavements were swept and there were very few people about.

Getting out of the car Cowley hit his leg, and let rip a ripe curse. They hadn't taken the chief's big limousine for this job and had picked up a squad car from the basement garage. Because it seemed they were tangling with hoods using a Jaguar, it seemed fitting they should use a Jaguar, also. Bodie's own car, a Lagonda that was not so much ancient as a venerable relic and by that token a marvel, remained in the garage of his Chelsea apartment. The two men eased toward Lewis's house.

In the shrubbery of Lewis's garden Jim Bain crouched down, moving only slowly, not disturbing the privet leaves. He held a Smith and Wesson .357 Magnum in his left hand, low. He felt a light touch on his back. He recognised the feel of that metallic touch through his jacket. Jim Bain remained very, very still.

Cowley moved through the shadows, around the side of Bain, and regarded him sorrowfully. Cowley's gun did not waver.

'You, Bain, are now dead.' The gun twitched, suddenly, horribly, a clear reminder. 'And Bain, you are slack. You are – '

Cowley didn't finish. A man's hard bulk slammed into him, upended him, twisted him around, knocked the gun away. A fist lifted in the half-light, wielding a gun, ready to slam the butt against Cowley's head.

Bodie stepped forward, busting a gut from containing his enjoyment.

'I told you you'd enjoy yourself, sir.'

Without moving in the grip of his attacker, Cowley said in his voice that lost all its plumminess and sounded like the contents of a gravel truck shifting: 'Well done, Wesley.'

Bill Wesley, Jim Bain's partner, recognising the set-up, began to lower the upraised gun.

'Very well,' said Cowley, 'done.'

As he spoke, smoothly, with the cunning expertise of long practice, Cowley reversed grips. Wesley crashed over into the ground. But, before he hit the ground, he went up in the air, and described an interesting circle, rotating – and then he hit the ground. He sat up, winded, trying to smile to enter into the spirit of the occasion.

These hard men were not play-acting. At any moment of the quick flurry of action – pseudo-action it never was – a gun could have gone off. Cowley knew that. Bodie knew that. These two C.I.5 men, Bain and Wesley, knew that. Training and experience and a continuous dedication alone would keep these men alive in other, similar, moments of real action.

The combat target course instructors marked you out as much on the targets you didn't shoot at as much as those you did. If you missed a shot at a villain – and were lucky – you might get a second bite at the cherry. There'd be no second chances if you put a couple of slugs through the guts of your partner because you shot before you'd properly identified the target.

Cowley looked at his three men. He nodded firmly, and turned to Bodie.

'You Bodie, I believe, mentioned something about a pure Malt Scotch?'

So Bodie and Cowley went back to their squad Jaguar to find a quiet spot to lubricate their working parts before heading back to H.Q. to find out what Doyle had turned up.

Fred, the commissionaire, even more alert now after his fracas with a hired hit-man, saw them through with a few quiet words. They went up in the lift to Cowley's office where after a few minutes they were joined by Doyle.

The tough ex-detective-constable shook his head over the state of Tin Can.

'He's not going to make it. He gave me a name – Huntley – pretends to be a Soho club-owner. Into anything that pays. He fixed up the raiders with Tin Can's services. Huntley was not inclined to be co-operative – '

At this Cowley lifted an eyebrow. Doyle rubbed his left palm absently over the knuckles of his right fist.

C.I.5 had to fight fire with fire.

'The raiders – four of them as we suspected – came down from the North – '

Cowley said: 'Where North? Germany? Sweden?'

Doyle smiled. 'I'll give you Huntley's exact words. He said: "Not North Pole North. North of England North." '

Cowley nodded. 'It fits.'

'Yes. You faked a positive ID. So why didn't they just filter away, run back abroad. We've got mug shots, makes, on a hundred killers. Arabs, Greeks, Africans. Does that bother them – when they're back home in their own back yard?'

'But these boyos *are* bothered,' said Cowley. 'They *need* to get rid of those witnesses.'

'Because they need to be able to go on working *here*.' Bodie let an exasperated puff of breath out. 'They're British – '

'And,' said Doyle. 'They don't have anywhere else to run to.'

Cowley moved to stand by the large-scale map of London. His dark gaze brooded on the mess of streets and squares and railway lines, a million hidey-holes.

'And they're not safe. They won't rest – not while any of our witnesses are still alive!'

Joe Q. Public had had a go at preventing what they thought was a bullion raid. The sham of that had not been leaked.

But now Cowley, riffling through the short list of witnesses and selecting Sumner as the best choice, fancied that Joe Q. Public would have a chance really to have a go – and this time without body contact. This time it would be C.I.5 who brought the muscle.

Cowley drove out to Sumner's riverside house, a nice place, bearing the marks of recent work, a place where an ex-Royal Marine who had hit lucky in the job stakes could be happy.

Sumner's dogs prowled as Cowley spoke to the still-fit ex-Marine.

'Look, I did five years in the Royal Marines – I stay fit – I'm alert. And I have a couple of Alsatian dogs –'

Cowley said: 'Then don't feed 'em.'

The sunshine threw dark shadows across the river as Sumner turned sharply to face Cowley. The flowers bloomed magnificently and a little breeze soughed through the surrounding trees.

'Are you trying to scare me?'

'No, Mr Sumner.'

'Should hope not. Tell you, the only thing gets me jittery is having those men of yours prowling through my shrubbery.'

'They're there for your protection.' Cowley paused. Then, speaking with heavy emphasis, he said: 'And I want to pull them out. I want to talk a deal with you, Mr Sumner. It's dangerous and it could be deadly.' Here Cowley smiled, and the smile changed and lit up his craggy face. 'But it shouldn't be too much for an ex-Marine who stays fit and alert.'

When Cowley assigned the various teams for the job, Bodie said: 'He's got to be crazy!'

Sharply, Doyle cut in with: 'He's got to be brave! Joe Public sticking his neck out for our benefit – and don't you forget that, Bodie.'

Bodie nodded. He was an aggressive tearaway, yes; but he shared Doyle's concern for innocent bystanders, in the tradition so rapidly created by Cowley. The news of Sumner's decision to dispense with police protection was spread. It hit the Street and filtered down through the layers of informants. The Police State, Big Brother is watching you syndrome worked in reverse. Cowley, confident in his men and yet still apprehensive over the ease with which the best laid plans could go wrong, set things in motion.

'Sumner's place is the easiest hit of all. It's isolated and remote down there by the river. The raiders have got to bite! Anyway, they'll know he shot the cine film. It's got to work.'

They drove down in the Hunter and parked well away, making their way to the overgrown garden with its spread of lawn trending down to the river under cover. Other C.I.5 men staked the area. Cowley brought his limousine down and stashed it away in a sideturning shrouded by overhanging trees. Here he set up the command H.Q.

Presently a pretty little bush growing in front of Sumner's house overlooking the sweep of lawn and the river spoke up fretfully.

'Doyle?' said the bush.

'Yeah?' said an adjacent bush.

'You forgot to bring any beer.'

'No I didn't. I remembered.'

'You did!' Great joy informed the bush's voice.

'Of course I did.' In his bush Ray Doyle was feeling a little guilty that he should be enjoying this. 'I remembered – not to bring any.' He waited the length of time he felt Bodie in his bush would take to react to this, and then said waspishly: 'It's not a party, Bodie. It's a stake-out.'

'I,' said Bodie wrathfully, 'am like a fine piece of machinery. I need lubrication.'

'Yeah, and too much lubrication and that fine piece of machinery will end up with a bullet up its crankcase.'

'One lousy beer.' Bodie felt the world was against him. 'It's nothing.'

'So you won't miss it, will you –'

This elevated exchange was interrupted as Cowley's voice came in on their headsets. They responded, still as alert as ever despite the badinage. They were professionals.

'We are in position about half a mile east of you. We're covering the approach road. Nothing can get through without us seeing it. Keep your radio open. I want to hear any and every thing.'

'Okay,' said Doyle.

'By the way,' went on Cowley. 'Tommy's covering the river.'

The partners said, as one: 'Tommy!'

Bodie parted the stems of his bush and glared towards the riverbank. He could see a rowboat there, with a bulky sack-covered object in the bows. He had no idea what that was. Tommy lay back in the boat, just visible, a mere part of the scenery from the lawn.

'What the hell is the old man up to?' fumed Bodie. He crabbed across to Doyle's bush and took cover. 'Tommy! He has got to be –'

'Bodie!' said Doyle.

' – start, staring raving bonkers! *He* sits out there a safe half mile away –'

'*Bodie!*' said Doyle.

' – and sends a psychopath in to keep *us* company. I'll tell you, Cowley is –'

Cowley's voice spluttered from the handsets.

'The radio is open, Bodie.'

Doyle lifted his spread hands to his ears. Now Bodie understood what his partner had been trying to tell him. Cowley went on grimly: 'But continue with your interesting assessment, Bodie. Cowley is . . . ? Cowley would like to know what Cowley is.'

Bodie stared at Doyle, and his eyebrows drew down. His face abruptly broke into a warm smile that would have melted a dozen virgin's hearts before breakfast. Very smoothly, Bodie said: 'Would you believe – warm and considerate?'

'For someone,' said Cowley, 'on stake-out, you talk too much.' The partners heard the change in the chief's voice as he said: 'And what are you lot grinning at?'

Doyle and Bodie understood that the agents with Cowley were getting it in the neck now. Served 'em right for grinning...

They tensed and then relaxed as Sumner appeared padding across the lawn to the garden shed. His instructions had been to carry on normally and that included lawning. He unlocked the shed and rolled out a lawnmower. He took only three tugs to start it and then, making a loud spluttering racket, he started off counter-marching up and down the lawn. Bodie and Doyle exchanged disgusted glances.

The warm smell of newly cut grass rose to mingle with the scent of flowers and rich earth, and the ever-present muddy, reedy, watery odours of the river.

Down in his rowboat Tommy McKay half-lifted, spotted the lawnmower, and sank down again. He felt very pleased with himself. At last Cowley had supplied him with a tool for the job that measured up to Shotgun Tommy's ideas on the subject.

This place was perfect for a hit, and there were killers roaming about ready to kill. Tommy just wanted to kill them first. It was not a lofty ambition. But it mattered.

Up at his road block with the C.I.5 men Cowley abruptly cocked his head. Through the racket of the lawnmower, drifting in very faintly, the throbbing of a car motor sounded.

There was no sign of a car on the road they guarded.

'Car,' said Cowley, staring back.

'Can't be,' said the nearest security man. 'There's no other road in – except –'

Cowley turned so fast the security man took a step back. '*Except?*'

'Well – there's a link road between Sumner's place and his neighbour. But there's no one there. The place is empty.'

'Empty! You fool!' Cowley saw it all – the raiders had got into the empty house and now they were on their way to Sumner's place. Cowley and his heavily-armed men were guarding nothing. 'Come on!' he bellowed, and leaped for the limousine.

Bodie and Doyle heard the car fitfully through the racket of the lawnmower. But the sound seemed to be coming from along the river. It faded and grew maddeningly. Tommy heard the engine noise. Sumner reached the end of the lawn and turned and switched the motor mower off. It racketted away to silence and in that hush the growing volume of noise from the river told the C.I.5 men where the menace was coming from.

Bodie leaped to his feet.

Doyle yelled into his radio: *'Boat!'*

The lawn was spacious. Bodie sprinted off with a yell: 'Get him under cover!'

He belted across the lawn towards Sumner. Tommy stayed in his boat but lifted up to stare up the river. Sumner, startled by the sudden apparition of a wild-looking fellow bedaubed with bits of leaves and twigs, springing from a bush, rushing straight at him, threw himself into a crouch.

Into his radio Doyle screamed: 'Hit! We're being hit!'

On the river an outboard motor boat creamed into view. Wide swathes of white water flared back. The two men in the boat stood looking at the lawn of Sumner's house. They saw Sumner moving away from a lawnmower, and abruptly swinging about, and they saw another man leap at Sumner.

Bodie, ready to drag Sumner to safety, was shattered to find the ex-Marine throwing punches. Bodie ducked and, so unexpected was the attack, half-slipped. He got an arm around Sumner's legs and pulled him down.

'Hold it, hold it!' bellowed Bodie. 'I'm on your side.'

The outboard motor boat raced down the river. Bodie got Sumner down. 'Keep down!' he shouted, and shoved Sumner's head into the freshly-cut grass.

Tommy started to paddle his boat out. He was awkwardly-placed; but he dug deeply with the oars, swinging the bows of the rowboat out towards midstream. The motorboat was fairly belting along now. The two men it contained opened up a rapid fire with sub machine-guns. The bullets gouged solidly into the lawn, plucking bits of grass stems up, gouging dark lines.

Doyle ran towards Bodie and Sumner firing his S&W.

The motorboat raced on, coming abreast of Tommy's little rowboat.

The look that transfigured Tommy's face would have baffled anyone who had no feeling for firearms. He reached forward and pulling the sack aside let his eyeline of vision pass along from the bows of the boat to the motorboat. Another moment – a tiny waiting fraction of time in which the chattering of the S.M.G.s shattered the silence – and then he jerked the lockstring.

The punt gun went off with a beautiful bang.

Designed to blow away fifty or sixty wildfowl in one discharge, a giant shotgun, the punt gun much used in the Fens of East Anglia, this was the weapon for Shotgun Tommy.

The closed fist of the packed shot barely had time to open out into the wildfowling pattern. They slugged solidly into the fragile scantlings of the motorboat. The boat crumpled as though it was a paper carton punched by a football fan. It shattered. The tank punctured. Petrol fumes rose.

With an almighty great kerrump the motorboat blew up. It brought a great smile of satisfaction and pleasure to the lean jawed face of Shotgun Tommy McKay.

Bits and pieces of the boat showered down. The surface of the water boiled. A massive concussion belted across the lawn and over the flower beds and bushes and blew in the front windows of Sumner's neat house. The smoke rose.

Shotgun Tommy regarded all this with the pleased grin of the fellow who has just rung the bell at the fair.

And yet – and yet he was still alive. The torture had not ended. There were other deaths, then, yet to come . . .

Doyle reached Bodie as the shock wave passed, taking his breath. He gave Sumner a helping hand to rise; but he was glaring at the river, and Tommy McKay and the rowboat and the devilish contraption in the bows.

'A cannon!' yelped Doyle. 'They've given the mad bastard a cannon!'

'A punt gun,' said Bodie. 'And I don't know who gave it to him – but I'm inordinately happy about it!'

Cowley's voice blasted from their radio handsets.

'Bodie! Doyle!' Cowley must have heard that bang. They must have heard it half-way to China. 'What's happening?'

'Nothing,' said Doyle. 'It's happened.' He looked down to the river where Tommy put a proprietal hand on the punt gun. God knew how much powder that thing gobbled up. 'Two raiders dead.' They were floating idly on the water, face down, drifting, trailing dark streams of blood. 'One busted boat.' That had to be so, for not a trace of the motorboat remained. 'One happy Tommy.' Even as he spoke, Doyle wondered how true that last was. Tommy McKay, happy? After what had happened to him?

'But,' put in Bodie, sourly. 'Otherwise okay.'

Between them the partners got Sumner back on his feet. He looked about, bewildered; but getting a grip on himself. The two raiders in the boat were dead. The sun shone. Bodie started to brush grass stems off Sumner, saying: 'And introductions are in order.'

The movement in the corner of his eye brought Bodie's head up, staring intently past the house. Instantly he stopped brushing Sumner off and knocked him full length back on to the grass.

Bodie hurled himself down over Sumner. Twisting as he fell, using Sumner as a fulcrum, Bodie swung his legs bodily. He caught Doyle behind the knees. His partner was swept off balance and tumbled down beside Bodie on the lawn.

The black Jaguar ghosted up to the house. The big bang was not fully understood by the raiders; but they leaped out of the car and advanced on the three men stranded in the middle of the lawn. The lawnmower afforded some cover and a barely discernible depression in the ground helped; but as the two raiders swung their S.M.G.s up it was clear that

Bodie, Doyle and Sumner were staked out.

The bursts of fire raking the lawn before them made it suicidal to lift their heads to risk a shot back.

They were done for, pinned down, unable to return fire . . .

Tommy saw.

He snatched up his partially sawn-off pump shotgun and leaped into the water, came wading, splashing and plunging towards the bank. His face was fixed, now, distant, a rictus of purpose transfixing those lean stubbled jaws, the fey light in his eyes baleful and charged with unholy joy.

Doyle saw him and yelled . . .

'Tommy! No!'

Shotgun Tommy reached the lawn and ran full tilt for the two raiders. The gunmen split their fire, and one sent a crashing fusillade of slugs that ripped into Tommy McKay. Bullets chewed across his chest and belly. But he kept on running. He kept on running. He lifted the shotgun.

He pulled the trigger and the blast blew the raider away, punching out his midriff, blowing it away in a welter of blood.

Tommy staggered and recovered. He was dead and he didn't know it. He started to swing the shotgun around towards the remaining gunman. The S.M.G. switched its fire from the men pinned on the lawn and snouted towards Tommy.

As one, Doyle and Bodie rose and fired, together, together . . .

Both their bullets, the .357 S&W Magnum and the 9 mm Browning hit the gunman in the left shoulder. He was spun about like a top, the S.M.G.s fire sprouting skywards.

Tommy aimed the shotgun. He was staggering, his legs spread, wavering, and the bullet wounds pocking his body and oozing . . .

'No, Tommy!' yelled Doyle. 'We want him alive!'

Tommy couldn't hear. He swung the shotgun up. He swung it up – up – up until it pointed at the sky, blue and high above. His eyes glazed. His finger contracted. Shotgun

Tommy fired his last shot, up at heaven, defiantly. Then his legs buckled and he collapsed, hit the ground, lay still.

With a single look at the badly-wounded raider, who sank to his knees, clasping his shattered shoulder, Bodie and Doyle ran like crazy men over to Tommy McKay.

When they reached the crumpled, pathetic body in its old blue jeans they could only stand, the guns useless in their fists, helplessly.

'He didn't have to do that,' Bodie said. 'Nobody asked him to do that.'

'He saved our hides,' said Doyle, choked, 'didn't he?'

Both partners turned to regard the sole remaining gunman. Aware of their regard he looked up, his face like the belly of a fish, his hand gripped on that shattered shoulder, shaking.

Doyle walked across. Very quietly, the vicious fury in him suppressed, Doyle said: 'Alive. You're alive. Because you're going to talk. You are going to tell us who hired you.'

As he spoke he suddenly reached out. He gripped the bullet-shattered shoulder. He squeezed. The raider screamed. The gunman dropped to his knees, shuddering. Doyle stared down at him, all the passions contained, controlled.

'Of course you are,' said Ray Doyle.

The Action Squad – the Big A – had wrapped up another one. It hadn't been theirs to start with. Perhaps, had it been, it wouldn't have ended like this.

Cowley walked along the line of blanket covered stretchers.

Ambulance men lifted one dead gunman and took him off. Next to him the form of Tommy, relaxed at last, lay on its stretcher. Two more ambulance men bent to take him away to the waiting ambulance, over past Sumner's pretty house.

'Don't,' said Doyle in a harsh, hating voice. 'Put him in the same wagon. Not with *them*!'

That tone of voice told the ambulance men that the speaker was very, very close to the edge. He looked tough, hard, vicious – but he was close to breaking point. They put the stretcher down and looked enquiringly at the chief.

Cowley nodded, so they picked up the water-soaked body of the next corpse and carried it away.

Speaking with a smoothness that he tried to make hard, matter-of-fact, Cowley said: 'I'll buy you a drink.'

Bodie brightened up. It would take something a great deal worse than this to affect Bodie.

'A pure Malt Scotch?' said Bodie.

Cowley regarded him gravely.

'Yes. Yes, I think you're ready for the hard stuff.'

And then, quite unexpectedly, Cowley put an arm around Doyle's shoulders. He spoke gruffly.

'And *you* need it.'

Walking along together, the three C.I.5 men left the scene of action.

But that scene would remain with them – they all knew that.

Chapter Five

Nesbit snugged the rifle into his shoulder and took careful aim through the scope. He did not particularly like the feel of the rifle – it was a Winchester model 190 and he had loaded it up with fifteen .22 Long Rifles – but, all the same it was a tool and in this modern decadent world of sin and horror a man with a true heart must use the modern devices of terror to overcome their more horrific counterparts.

Dawn whispered gently about him and an early breeze rustled through the trees and bushes in which he had concealed himself. The country was pretty wild up here. The target he had laid out was a good distance off, and Nesbit was aware with a painful flush of pleasure that this test would demand his best.

He wanted to make sure the targeted device would work and then he could go ahead. And he particularly did not want to be late for work today. So he snugged the Winchester into his shoulder and peered through the telescopic sight and when he had ironed out his breathing and steadied the image, let fly.

He missed with the first two shots, and adjusted the scope fractionally each time. Even as he pressed the trigger for the third time he knew he had scored a bull. The .22 Long Rifle whammed dead square into the target attached to Nesbit's device.

Feeling that the day was his, Nesbit sat up and waited. He had set the device for only a short delay, all that was necessary to make sure his brilliant idea would work. After a minute the device exploded with a little spurt of flame, a handful of wafted smoke. Moments later the blast reached Nesbit under the trees.

He smiled.

An inconspicuous-looking man, the sort of fellow you wouldn't look at twice, who would appear to have – even if he did not – a thinning hairstyle, silver-rimmed glasses and a runny nose. You'd never notice him.

Stowing his gear back into the duffle bag Nesbit went across to his four-year-old Escort, unlocked the door and climbed in. He drove the car carefully. Susan was waiting for him just past the big sign at the end of the reservoir where the birds clucked and chattered. The sign read:

WORLD CHEMICAL PRODUCTS –
SPORTS AND SOCIAL CLUB

The moment Nesbit's Escort hove into view past the end of the reservoir Susan stepped towards it. She was shaking. Her pretty face, usually vapid with wonder at the world, was now tensed and drawn, the lines in her skin marked. She hurried towards Nesbit as he stopped the car and pulled on the handbrake.

Nesbit got out, locked the door, and then taking Susan's elbow in his left hand ran her back into the concealment of the weatherbeaten buildings sagging beside the reservoir. Susan panted. Her neat office dress was rumpled, untidy. She lifted her hand and jangled the shiny keys on their ring. She didn't say anything yet; but she ran the tip of her tongue over her parched lips.

Nesbit smiled. He took the keys and pocketed them.

Before he could move, Susan grabbed his wrist and glared into his eyes. She was shaking.

'Now what about me? You promised me!'

Nesbit, with that sly smile plastered on his face, produced a roll of tissue and unwound it to reveal a small hypodermic. Susan snatched it, panting, rolled her sleeve up with the quick frantic movements of a hunted animal in a hedgerow.

Nesbit showed his distaste, for he was a fastidious man in most things.

'At least sterilise the needle.'

He took out his lighter, it had been given to him by his mother who was now dead, an event he could not recall without fresh and torturing pain, and shamefacedly Susan flipped the needle through the flame.

'I need it. I really need it.'

Nesbit snapped the lighter shut. He studied the girl for a moment and then nodded, satisfied. 'Yes,' he said, and walked away to his car. He started off and drove away without looking back. Anyway, Susan was no longer partaking of mundane reality.

The complex of buildings and plant stretched over a good few acres of what had once been desolate moorland. Nesbit went into work, showing his pass, parking his car, donning his white coat. He had no trouble. He chose the staff coffee-making machine on a corridor intersection of the main block, with glass-walled offices stretching away each side and an emergency exit handy.

No one took any notice of the familiar daily routine of having the coffee-making machine reloaded. He did that with the instant coffee and then when a lull in the passing office workers gave him all the time he needed he used another of Susan's keys to unlock the water container. Moving with precision he used an eye-dropper and plopped out just three shining globules of the colourless fluid. When he closed up and walked away he was smiling again.

Customers for the morning coffee reduced the level of water in the coffee maker. Miller, chief of the biological division, always drank it black and his pretty secretary provided him with a cup before the morning board meeting.

In the board meeting the polished, scrubbed, immaculately-dressed administrators rubbed shoulders with the white-coated chemists. They were waiting for Miller, for the first item on the agenda concerned his division. They waited.

Finally, Harvey, the big boss, said doubtfully: 'The main

item this morning needs Miller – without him . . . '

As though on cue the door opened and Miller entered. He did not look about cheerfully, as he usually did. His face wore an odd expression.

Not noticing, brisk, wanting to get on, Harvey said: 'Ah, Mr Miller, perhaps now we can begin.'

Miller just stood. The early sunlight from the open window threw odd shadows across Miller's face.

Harvey spoke up, puzzled. 'Miller?' Then: 'Ted?'

The others around the table looked across. Miller was acting most strangely . . .

'Ted?'

Miller smiled foolishly. He staggered, lurching to one side. As though unable to regain his balance, impelled by some inner compulsion that gave him the wings of an angel, he suddenly ran full tilt across the room.

Before anyone could do anything, Ted Miller raced across the board room and dived out of the open window.

It was a long drop to the concrete below.

After the witnesses to the 'Tunnel Approach Bullion Raid' had been reassured that the danger was over, Cowley decided to sharpen up some of the members of his team. Three hoods had been killed, and Shotgun Tommy had at last found that surcease from pain he had craved for so long. Cowley determined to get C.I.5 back to full fighting strength *tout de suite* – and the tooter, as Bodie put it, the sweeter.

They travelled up to a remote area in an unspecified part of England where they were run through their paces to the sadistic enjoyment of various gathered experts. Target practice, body-contact combat, obstacle courses, weapon and explosive and electronic recognition – these men of C.I.5 were kept busy.

Out on the range with a hint of a nip in the air, Bodie and Doyle were happily banging away with handguns, each using an identical weapon, trying one to outshoot the other. Although Ray Doyle was the noted handgun expert, Bodie being the rifleman of the outfit, there was little to choose between them as they rapped off their six, ejected, slammed in fresh shells and swung once more into the stance to blast away again. The man-shape targets shuddered and jumped and looked in one hell of a mess.

When the next clump of six had been shot off each and the air stopped quivering, Tony Bastable wandered over, swinging his Colt Python from a forefinger. He was always called Tony, and was a new man, learning the ways of C.I.5, hoping to pass through all the tests and be assigned a partner and a job.

He swung suddenly into the stance, square on to the target, legs bent, crouching, both hands locked, finger on trigger and staring down the sights. He cut loose.

The partners watched him critically.

'Not bad,' said Bodie. 'If the target had been slimming lately he'd have missed with a couple.'

'You were slow opening up, Tony,' said Doyle, severely. Both he and Bodie liked to take the mickey out of Tony, who was nearing twenty-seven, too damned handsome for his own good, and transparently eager. 'It don't always pay to go into the stance, no matter what regulations say. Like we told you.'

Bodie nodded. 'Regulations say a police marksman with a rifle must always fire from the shoulder and use the sights. Well, Tony, we're not police. We're C.I.5. Sometimes you have to cut corners.'

'Not, Bodie, whilst I am within earshot!'

Cowley's voice cut them up, bringing them around smartly. The chief strode across the range, coat flapping, so they knew something had blown up. Cowley told them.

'World Chemical Products. Man just fell out of a tenth storey window.'

Doyle said: 'That's police business.'

'He jumped.'

Bodie said: 'That's his business.'

'Somebody had slipped him a drug – him and half the staff there.'

Doyle and Bodie, together, said: 'That's Drug Squad business.'

Cowley regarded them down his nose. 'What are you – some kind of Music Hall act?'

Young Tony Bastable stood to one side drinking all this in.

Bodie summed it up. 'Whatever we are – sir – *you made us.*'

With Tony trailing, they turned and walked back from the range. Doyle said the obvious: 'Why us?'

'Because the dead man had a Class XA Security Rating – and that puts him right under *our* umbrella.'

Tony hopped about in the rear, and finally managed to blurt out: 'What about me, sir? Can I –'

Cowley half-turned. The urgency of the situation demanded immediate action. But he said as gently as he could: 'Not yet, Tony. Finish up here. Your turn will come pretty soon now.'

The C.I.5 men lost no time in making the journey to World Chemical Products and they arrived to find the chaos continuing. People wandered about lost in private dreams. Young girls were particularly susceptible; laughing and crying at the same time, they cluttered the place with horror that bordered on the farcical. But the C.I.5 men knew the time for jokes had gone – with Miller dead, with other people in hospital, with drugs circulating within the whole area and knocking people over like flies in autumn. They set about checking over possible sources.

Harvey, the big boss, retained his senses, as did his secretary, although her eyes were swollen from crying. News came through that a girl had died in hospital. It was clear to the C.I.5 men that drugs had been administered here, causing the chaos and death. They began asking questions.

Doyle told Harvey: Those people out there and in hospital are under the influence of drugs.'

'But how administered?' said Bodie. 'You appear to be okay. So what was it they drank, or ate –'

'Or breathed –' put in Doyle.

'That you didn't?' finished Bodie.

Harvey's secretary sniffled and said: 'Coffee.'

She explained. 'Mr Harvey and I dislike coffee. But there are coffee-making machines on every floor –'

'Close 'em all down, quick,' snapped Doyle. 'We'll have the water and the coffee and the very guts of the machines analysed –'

'We can do that here,' offered Harvey. 'We are a chemical company with analytical chemists –'

'Do it!' said Bodie.

During the time the analysis was prepared Bodie and Doyle carried on their investigations. The person responsible for the coffee-making machines, Susan Green the catering manageress, had been seen to leave World Chemicals looking ill. The partners arranged to have the reports radioed to them via Cowley and took off. Halfway to Susan Green's apartment the radio in the car spluttered and Cowley's voice came in.

'The water in the coffee machine had been laced all right. A.D.X.'

'A.D.X.,' said Doyle. 'That figures.'

'A.D.X.!' said Bodie, filled with disgust and rage.

'Worse than L.S.D.,' said Doyle.

'L.S.D. to the power of ten.' Cowley's voice carried the grimness they all felt.

'Somebody,' said Bodie, 'doesn't like machine-made coffee – and that's just about everybody.'

'Yeah,' said his partner. 'Don't you wish it was just that?'

'It frightens the pants off me. And I like to choose when I expose my legs to the air. A few drops of tasteless fluid . . . They could pit it anywhere. Have you thought about that?'

'Bodie. I *am* thinking about that.'

Miss Susan Green's apartment was situated in a pleasant block with shade trees whose leaves still retained much of their summer green. The place felt quiet and refined. Doyle pulled the Hunter up and he and Bodie alighted as a man

57

hurried down the front steps of the apartment block. He drew the usual quick interrogative stare the agents gave everyone with whom they came into contact — a smartly-dressed man in a light topcoat, about thirty — but they could not see his face. Doyle slammed the Hunter's door and followed Bodie up into the building.

They got no answer to the door buzzer of Miss Green's apartment. Presently, using a picklock, Bodie eased his way in. Susan sprawled on a sofa, wearing a lounging robe, her legs apart, her body relaxed, dreamy. The place presented just the right appearance of a smart young career lady's apartment.

At once both agents sensed a wrongness about that atmosphere.

'Susan Green, isn't it?' began Bodie most engagingly. 'No, don't get up. We missed you at World Chemicals. You were upset, distraught, we're told — well, *anyone* would have been upset after what happened there today.' He smiled. 'It was the coffee vending machines, you know. The ones you hold the keys for.'

'I – I had nothing to do with it.'

'We didn't suggest you did. Who had access to the keys?'

'Well – I – they hang in my office.'

'No.' Bodie's smile was warm and generous. 'No. We are assured you always carry them with you. And – ' Here Bodie took her purse from the walnut side-table and upended it, scattering a mixed collection of oddments out. He held the keys aloft. ' – you see, our information was correct.'

'Look – I'm very tired. Tomorrow? I'm really very tired – '

Doyle moved forward. 'Aren't you, though. How long have you been popping?'

Bodie threw a startled glance at his partner. He hadn't suspected – but Ray Doyle had served his time with the Drug Squad. Doyle took Susan's arm and lifted the sleeve. He grunted. The arm was a mess. 'Long enough – almost run out of veins! We'd better take her in.'

'No ... please ...'

Bodie started to heave her to her feet and realised at once her deadweight limpness. Doyle snorted. 'She's tripping right now. We've struck gold. A girl with a habit – and the keys to the coffee vending machines.'

'Yeah,' said Bodie. 'That habit. They'll do anything . . . '

Bodie began to look around the apartment and soon found a hypo and a twist of paper, which he opened, and offered to Doyle.

Doyle gave it only the most perfunctory of tests. He was sure, as sure as he'd ever been. Susan lay on the sofa where Bodie dropped her. She was already looking bad.

'This hasn't been cut,' said Doyle, and the urgency in his voice brought Bodie around. 'It's pure one hundred per cent. Somebody sent her on a *one way* trip!'

Bodie started for the phone. 'Ambulance!'

Doyle was fretting over something else as they did what they could to make Susan comfortable before the ambulance came. She was already sliding away into her own cotton-wool dreamland from which she might never return. It was clear that she'd only just taken the fix before the two C.I.5 men called. Doyle looked up, suddenly, and his face abruptly took on the look of a hunting wolf.

'I must be crazy!'

'You won't,' said Bodie. 'Get any argument from me.'

'When we arrived there was a man just leaving. Didn't see his face. But there was something familiar – the walk, the hairline – not sure – but I *am* sure it was Eric Sutton.'

'Eric Sutton?'

'A pusher!'

Bodie started to speak and Doyle cut in. 'You stay with her.' Doyle belted for the door. 'She might talk when she comes round – *if* she comes round.'

Chapter Six

The between-hours drinking club presented a gloomy, secretive appearance, badly lit by artificial light so that the customers might be spared the sight of the cockroaches fandangoing behind the bar. The place was sleazy. Not above half a dozen seedy customers were propping up the bar, drinking gloomily, when Doyle arrived. His first act was to yank out the plug of the juke box, silencing the row and effectively obtaining complete attention. He displayed his ID. His pointing finger travelled along the line of shrinking customers, and settled on the man he wanted.

'You!'

The fellow – he was a lean lanky fellow with long hair and a scrub of beard, wearing jeans – split. He tried to make a run for it. Doyle caught him, slammed him against the bar and frisked him. He came up with a wicked-looking flick knife.

'Nice,' said Doyle.

'It's a plant,' the man whined. He appealed to the other customers. 'You saw him. A plant –'

The other customers had their own troubles. They had no wish at all in the whole wide world to tangle with the law.

'We,' said Doyle, 'should have a private chat.' He fished out a tenpenny piece and hurled it in the general direction of the barman. He thumb-gestured towards the juke-box. 'Play something loud.'

Then he pushed the jean-clad scruff into the back room.

The odour of over-ripe cheese, of ancient wine, of rotten

wood puffed up in the little space. Doyle stuck out his arm and swept a row of tins on to the floor. They made a splendid din. He kicked a wooden crate, sending it crashing heavily over the grimy linoleum. The scrub-bearded man in the faded jeans picked up a big two-gallon tin that had once held something edible – the label had long-gone but the smell lingered – and hurled it against the wall. The crashes sounded ominously loud.

Then the bearded scrub said: 'What do you want, Doyle?'

'Information. Eric Sutton.'

'Look, Doyle. I'm not big time like you. Just the drug run. But Sutton – you can't touch Sutton. We're getting ready setting him up for the big pounce.'

'I'm C.I.5 now, Benny. C.I.5 can touch him.' Doyle threw a tin at the wall. 'I'm talking about world class now, Benny. I need Sutton.'

'Damn,' said Benny. 'Been setting him up for months.'

'After I've used him – you can have him for murder.'

Benny brightened. 'Murder? That'll be nice. I'll find him for you, Doyle.'

Doyle turned to leave and Benny said: 'Hey – aren't you forgetting something?'

'I'll be in touch – oh – ' He realised what Benny was on about. He cocked his head to one side. 'Where?'

'Have to be somewhere it shows . . . ' Then Benny groaned. 'And I've got a date tomorrow!'

'Sorry, Benny,' said Doyle, and drew back and let rip with a roundhouse that connected splat along Benny's cheek. Benny dropped. Doyle looked down at him.

'And thanks.'

Bodie saw Susan Green into the Intensive Care unit of the hospital. She looked pale and fragile, surrounded by the medical apparatus, saline drips, tubes pulsing, screens, oxygen apparatus on hand, and Bodie shook his head. Cowley arrived and stood looking down, grim and angry. 'Will she live?'

'God knows.'

'Yes,' said Cowley. 'But unfortunately I haven't been in touch with Him for some time. What do the doctors say?'

'Well, if this was a horse race, she'd be a rank outsider.'

'She's said nothing? No – well, we do know why the A.D.X. was put in the coffee machine. The demand arrived on the P.M.'s desk an hour ago.'

Bodie felt the resigned anger, the futile anger. 'Pay up – or else?'

'Wish it was. No, this is idealism – or pseudo-idealism. God save us from all idealists, idealists of this stripe.'

'I thought,' said Bodie, 'you and He weren't talking.'

A sudden fierce flare of pain knifed through Cowley's bad leg. He gripped down, hard, fighting the agony. 'Oh,' he said in a voice almost steady. 'He does me the occasional favour.'

'What *do* they want?' Bodie ignored the chief's distress. Cowley would cut him to pieces if he tried to offer sympathy.

Cowley said, quoting from memory: 'Cease manufacture of chemicals for biological warfare and destroy all stocks – '

'Signed?'

'Not signed.'

'Deadline?'

'No deadline.'

'A nutty idealist?'

'I – I'm not sure. One thing is sure. He'll make his point more than once if we don't nail him.' Cowley looked down on Susan. 'She's a pretty little thing. See what you can make of her. I'm going to run a check on reservoirs.'

'Reservoirs!'

'Beats coffee-vending machines – and this character is thinking big.'

Whilst Cowley set about checking the reservoirs he figured likely targets and arranging for men to be stationed there, using with C.I.5 authority uniformed and plainclothes men from all over, Betty, his ravishing secretary, walked into his office quickly, her colour high. Cowley looked up.

'An anonymous phone call – a Second Demonstration of Strength was what he said –'

The reports confirmed the efficacy of the demonstration. A pub had been the target. The beer engine had been laced with A.D.X. At closing time the results had been spectacular – and ghastly. The pile up involved cars and lorries, motor cyclists and the police cars that raced to the scene. Smashed wrecks littered the roadway as drugged drivers drove madly along, uncaring, creating havoc.

Cowley listened in a stony silence. At the end he pushed back in his seat, gripping his bad leg, his face like granite.

'Here,' he said, 'endeth the second lesson.'

The day wore on. Bodie stuck with Susan, trying to make sense of her unco-ordinated ramblings, getting nowhere. Cowley organised what cover he could for the reservoirs. His nose told him they were the obvious choice for a man who wanted to hold a city to ransom. If he only knew which one! And Ray Doyle took the call from Benny, the undercover cop, and met him at the stage door of the Rex.

Doyle parked the Hunter half on the kerb and walked across. The back alley blew with discarded papers and cigarette packets, a stray dog slunk along and the smell resembled that of Dracula's ancestral grave. 'In there?' Doyle nodded to the door with its peeling paint set in grey crumbling brickwork.

'Yeah – but wait, Doyle. On what they pay us we'll never be millionaires, right?'

'Right.'

'And the public abuses us, and, any day we're likely to get our legs – or more tender parts – blown off, right? So we should get *some* fun, right?' He checked his watch. 'So wait a couple of minutes.'

Mystified, anxious to get on, Doyle regarded Benny. The undercover cop sported a big bruise on his cheek.

'Afternoon strip show for the dirty raincoat brigade. Curtain down in about a minute. Eric Sutton's in there, dropping off a little packet of Big H to a good customer –'

63

'So we catch him.'

'So we catch him – but after curtain down, right? After curtain down the dressing rooms will be crawling with – '

' – birds.'

Benny smiled happily. 'Birds. Birds in singular states of disarray. Birds with very few feathers indeed. Wait a couple of minutes.'

Very definitely, Ray Doyle said: 'Wait a couple of minutes.'

'This,' said Benny, smiling, 'is my favourite bust. Always – just about this time.'

Doyle moved closer to the door. He could hear faint music, bump and grind music. After a few moments that stopped and a scatter of perfunctory applause reached him. He cocked an eye at Benny. Happily, Benny stood up and nodded. Together, they moved to the stage door and went inside.

The girls from the last set-scene on stage were just streaming back to the dressing rooms. Doyle blinked. Benny stood just inside the door, his hands hanging limply at his sides, and he stared happily. Birds . . . Brilliant birds, long of slender leg, narrow of waist, rounded of thigh, voluptuous, enticing, mouth-watering, gorgeous birds. There was no need to look closely at them, not too closely, not so close that the paint and the powder and the feathers failed to conceal what this life was all about.

The girls in a great colourful chattering tide moved back to the dressing rooms. Their flesh glowed in the dusty lighting. Then, following them, walked a stripper who carried her bra swinging in one hand, anxiously, her G-string miniscule, her legs more shiny than powdered. Her face looked tight. Her mouth pinched in. She needed no eye-shadow.

Eric Sutton pushed upright from where he had been leaning negligently against the wall. Fly-blown posters advertising long-gone shows, the sounds of the girls going into the dressing room, the music blatting muted from out front, the taste of ancient dust in the air – Sutton smiled. The lights shone down on his smart clothes, the immaculately coiffed head of dark oiled hair, the glint of gold at fingers and wrist.

'You were great, Pam. Just great – '

The stripper halted, rocking on her high heels. 'Did you bring my stuff?' Her lips glistened, ripe, bruised.

Sutton produced a small – a very small bouquet of flowers. They were forget-me-nots. They looked shockingly out of place. Pam put out her hand for the bouquet, and Sutton withdrew the flowers, smiling. Pam pushed her hand down into the G-string and fumbled out a tightly-wadded pack of notes. How she'd kept them there remained her secret. Sutton, smiling, confident, very much the Valentino, took the notes and extended the flowers.

A hard hand clamped his wrist. He was swung about almost off balance.

Benny clapped the cuffs on one wrist with expert ease and continued to pivot Sutton around so that he almost collided with Doyle.

'He's all,' said Benny, snapping the other cuff. 'Yours.'

Sutton recovered his balance and his poise. He was a man who remained cocksure of himself, even when Benny broke open the packet concealed in the flowers. 'A plant,' he said. 'Pam – you saw him plant that?'

The stripper looked ghastly; but she shook her naked shoulders and whispered: 'Yes. Yes, I saw him . . . '

She spoke as though the two lines she'd been given had cost money; but Doyle felt the quick and savage spurt of anger and sorrow for her. Benny had no need to say: 'Pam would say anything to keep her supply going.'

Sutton shrugged his shoulders in that smart coat and shook the handcuffs. 'So what charge?'

Doyle smiled at him. 'No charge.'

The words and the smile made only the smallest impression on Sutton. He held up his cuffed hands. 'I know the score. No charge, no cuffs, nothing.'

The planned bust of this pusher and his sources had been upset; but Benny found he was beginning to enjoy this scene even more – and with birds! He said: 'That's if you're dealing with the police. But – he's not the police.'

5

'Not police . . . Then what?'

Doyle cut in, explaining everything and explaining nothing.

'C.I.5!'

Doyle started to remove Sutton, who still looked toughly uncompromising, beginning to suss out the implications of C.I.5. Doyle glanced back. Pam looked shrunken, holding her dangling bra to her, her face pinched. 'Benny?' said Doyle.

'Someone should stay, don't you think? And help? And – case the joint?'

Doyle nodded, turned and pulled Sutton out. Benny turned the other way, looking about, smiling happily.

'My favourite bust,' said Benny.

Bodie kept a close watch on Susan Green. With skilled medical care she was not going to die, that at least he could be thankful for. But pure medicine however devoted was not going to get through to her, to unravel the secrets she held, to provide some clue to the instigator. Bodie could do that, if he was lucky, if he was devoted himself, if he handled it just right.

The nurse checked Susan's pulse, calm and competent and only slightly put out by the male presence of Bodie, sitting watchfully at the bedside. The smell of hospitals usually turned a man off, but, sometimes, they had the reverse effect. This man – his name was Bodie – with his immaculate but tasteful clothes, his lean, hard, virile face and body, the sureness with which he held himself – the nurse came back to her charge as Susan moaned.

Instantly Bodie leaned forward. 'Susan – Susan . . .'

Susan moaned again and flung out her hand which encountered Bodie's. She gripped. She gripped as though Bodie's hand was the last lifebelt on the *Titanic*.

'George?'

'I'm here, Susan – right here beside you.'

It was a chance – Susan's eyes flickered open. She gazed painfully at Bodie.

66

'George?' Then, as Bodie smiled encouragingly, she said with a gasping effort: 'You can't be. George was my cat. White – Persian.' She stared, and Bodie saw she was still under the influence, not here at all. 'Had to have him put down.' Then, with a sudden abrupt change of emotion. 'No! No – it wasn't my fault!'

Quickly, Bodie cut in: 'Tell me about him.'

The nurse stepped forward, saying: 'That's enough – '

Bodie ignored her. He grasped Susan's hand. 'You've *got* to tell me about him.' He bent closer. 'D'you hear me, Susan? I want to know about George.'

She rolled her eyes, her face twisting. Relentlessly, Bodie went on: 'I ran over him in my car.' Susan's face shone with sweat; but the nurse did not bend to wipe it away. Bodie said: 'I heard his bones crack. But he wasn't dead so I had to reverse and run over him again.'

Susan's head began to shake from side to side on the pillow. Her fair hair slicked with sweat. 'No! Oh, no . . No . . . '

She burst into sobs, shaking, sobbing, almost choking, and the nurse, held in a stasis of horror, could do nothing as Bodie said: 'That's better . . . Much better.' He wiped a strand of hair from her forehead. Susan half-sat up. As though it was the most natural thing in the world Bodie took her in his arms, enfolding her, holding her close. 'Cry, Susan. Cry it out.'

Over the shoulder of the sobbing girl in his arms, Bodie's gaze met that of the nurse, white-faced, shocked. But on that face a glimmering of admiration for Bodie showed, peeping through. Both of them knew this was the breakthrough for Susan.

The interrogation room at C.I.5 presented a bleak and unpleasant appearance. Eric Sutton sat backwards on a bentwood chair cuffed through the rungs. He sneered at Cowley and Doyle.

'Oh, you're experts. I can see that. But it won't do you any good. You'll get nothing out of me, except a counter-suit in court. I've been worked over by experts before.' He abruptly jerked his head down and tweaked off that immaculate oiled black hair. A naked scalp showed under the lights, hideously scarred. 'Experts from *my* side of the fence did that. D'you think you can succeed where they failed?'

Cowley nodded his head at Doyle and they left the interrogation room. Cowley said: 'He's a pusher?'

'Not big, not small. Medium time.'

'But he preys on human frailty. If you prey on it you have to know it, understand it. *Fear it.*'

When they re-entered the interrogation room Cowley was fully prepared. He looked down on Sutton and said: 'Names. Do you hear me, Mr Sutton? We need a name.' Cowley spoke pleasantly, and as he spoke so he produced a hypodermic needle. 'I don't suppose you fought in the war – any war – Mr Sutton? I've fought in several. The worst was against a – barbaric race. But the British are nothing if not adaptable. We learn barbarism very quickly. We had a problem one day. Was the road ahead mined? Our prisoners wouldn't talk.'

Here Cowley moved the syringe so the glass caught the light.

'So we bound them and made them lead the advance. They didn't think we would, not at first. But then – the first man up ahead was – ' Cowley snapped his fingers. ' – gone.' He snapped his fingers again. 'Anti-personnel mines, Mr Sutton. Very nasty. The second man. The third man. *Then* they talked. *Then* they knew we meant it.'

Cowley stood up. Sutton's gaze remained glued to the hypo.

'A shocking story, Mr Sutton. It still shocks me. But it was necessary – to save hundreds of lives it was necessary. I am now talking in hundreds of thousands. I am willing to be shocked again – if necessary.'

Susan had slept and now Bodie could talk to her with a hope

she would understand what he was saying. He held her hand.

' . . . those people in World Chemicals. Like George, they died. The girl, she died of an overdose. She was just eighteen. And you, Susan, you very nearly died.' He paused and then spoke with deep meaning. 'Because *they* wanted you dead.'

'It wasn't my fault . . . not my fault . . . '

'No – but it will be if it goes on. Thousands of people, dead – but you can save them, Susan. If you want to.' She responded with a surprised stare, struggling up through the waves of coloured cotton-wool fogging her mind. 'Names,' said Bodie. 'I need a name.'

A further ultimatum had been received by the Prime Minister. Cowley took the information in grim-faced, and went back to Sutton.

He resumed where he had left off. And this time the force of his anger was barely contained.

'I am going to hoist you with our own petard, Mr Sutton.' He squirted the hypo and bent to the cuffed man. 'I am going to turn you into an addict. A crash course in addiction – we have access to the purest stuff. A craving, crawling, do anything junkie. Look into my eyes, Mr Sutton.' As Sutton attempted to turn away, Cowley grabbed his fancy lapels and dragged his head up. 'Look! Remember the road that was mined. Do you have any doubt at all that I intend doing what I say?'

Quite matter-of-factly, Cowley told Doyle: 'Roll up his sleeve.'

Doyle moved forward.

Sutton tried to curl into a ball. 'No! No . . . '

Taking no notice, Cowley and Doyle prepared to inject Sutton. The pusher shrieked, writhing, trying to drag away.

'No! No!' Then. in a frantic outburst, gobbling with passion: 'It was Nesbit! Nesbit!'

At that moment in the intensive care unit Bodie, patiently

talking to Susan, at last heard her say in a weak, breathy voice: 'Nesbit . . . '

The Jaguar screeched around corners and hared along the roads, belting like a bat out of hell for Charles Nesbit's house.

'We have until half past five,' said Cowley. 'That was the time of the ultimatum. Unless a public announcement is made that all biological warfare research has been renounced – a major city starts getting a gallon of A.D.X.'

After a time, when they had digested that sobering information Doyle said – carefully – 'He might have a point, sir. Be a good thing if –'

'Research,' snapped Cowley, 'doesn't automatically mean aggression. We have to find means of defence. TB doctors don't seek to propagate TB, do they?'

Another silence. Cowley and Doyle watched the road. Then Doyle asked a question which, the second it was out of his mouth, he wished he hadn't asked. He thought he understood a little of George Cowley, chief of C.I.5, and so he thought he knew the answer. He asked: 'Would you have done it, sir? Sutton?'

Cowley gave him one glance, and then went back to his radio, checking out the guards at the reservoirs.

Cowley and Doyle in the Jaguar rounded the penultimate corner and began to slow so as to stop before they reached Nesbit's road. The houses ranked to either hand, discreet, suburban, dozing. As the Jaguar slowed an old Lagonda kept in perfect condition, tuned, speedy, shot into view from the other direction. It slowed. The two cars halted together, facing each other.

From the Jaguar Cowley and Doyle jumped out.

From the Lagonda Bodie leaped out.

The three men met midway.

Bodie and Doyle, together, said: 'How did you get here?'

Cowley said: 'Never mind how for now.' He nodded towards the house. 'Nesbit!'

70

A rifle shot blasted from the privet bushes fronting the house.

The C.I.5 men broke instantly for cover.

The rifle shots blammed – small calibre stuff. But the .22 Long Rifles slashed into the tyres of the Jaguar and the Lagonda. The cars sank down. Guns in their fists the C.I.5 men sprinted from cover to cover along the street, heading for Nesbit's house. Before they reached it an Escort whipped out of the garage, span on shrieking tyres, hared away up the street.

Cowley span, headed back limping for the cars. He was shouting as he went.

'That's the bastard! Get those wheels changed! Move!'

Over the radio he quickly ordered an A.P.B. on Nesbit, and road blocks, and then slammed the handset back and limped back up the drive and into Nesbit's house. He was impolite to the front door, and it sagged back from a shattered lock. He barged inside, furious, seeking some kind of lead.

Cowley turned over a number of rooms, progressing through the living room, the kitchen, up the stairs, the spare room, until he came to Nesbit's bedroom. He stood in the doorway and looked about, and half of the unanswered questions came clear.

Not that that was of much use. He'd known he was dealing with a nutter, for all the high-faluting fol-de-rol about idealism. The usual posters were pasted up; Revolution – yes, well you could buy those along Oxford Street. The truckle bed was shoved into an alcove. The posters about that – BAN WHITE BREAD – PROTECT THE OZONE – BRING BACK THE BEAVER – indicated a crankiness to Nesbit's character, although nothing intrinsically was wrong with the stated aims – or most of them. It seemed to Cowley, looking about, that Nesbit spent most of his time here. They were getting a make out on him now; but he wouldn't be known, that was for sure. A nutter, a crank, deciding to hold a city to ransom. Cowley's job was to stop that. Once Nesbit had been stopped then others could argue the pros and cons.

In the corner and propped so they stuck into a sharp angle of the alcove a pair of water skis looked new, and yet well-used. There were books piled about them, and a raffle of sportsman's gear. Doyle came in, still wiping his hands.

'Yeah,' he said. 'A sportsman. He can shoot, I'll give the bastard that.'

A packet of red, white and blue targets had been torn open and tossed down on to a cluttered table.

Bodie came in, swearing about the damage to his own Lagonda.

Cowley looked at his watch. 'It's four o'clock.'

'That means,' said Doyle. 'We have an hour and a half –'

'No,' said Cowley. 'Less than that if I'm to advise the P.M. to make his announcement to meet this madman's terms. We can't leave it until the last minute. We can't take that chance. An hour – an hour at most. Then we have to give him what he wants.'

'And open the floodgates to every nut in the country!' Bodie glared around the cluttered, untidy room. On a bench under the window chemical apparatus glittered, prickly with sharp chemical colours. Doyle followed his partner's gaze, and then looked on past the packet of targets, past the toppling piles of books, past the cricket bat and the water skis and the deflated rugby ball – Doyle let out a sharp exclamation. He darted across the room and hauled the water skis out.

'Water skis! That girl –'

Bodie knew, instantly. 'Susan! She had a pair of water skis too!'

The Jaguar carried them back to the hospital, with Doyle's foot on the floor, bellowing with power. In the intensive care unit Susan smiled wanly up at Bodie, alarmed by the presence of two other grim-faced men, glowering down. Bodie waved them back. He bent and smiled, and told her what he wanted to know.

'Water skis – ?'

'You have a pair – he has a pair –'

'Well, yes. That is how we met, at the World Chemical's sports club. I believed him – I don't know who invited him – but I –' Her fair hair was still damp.

'Where did you ski together?'

'At the sports club, of course. On the reservoir –'

The three hard men were out of the room with a silent, feral burst of speed that made the nurse blink.

Time ticked by, seeming to go faster and faster as the deadline approached. Cowley fretted. 'It's a long shot.' He needn't have said that, but he said it, anyway.

And Ray Doyle had no need to say: 'Let's face it, sir. It's our *only* shot.' But he said that, anyway...

They drove.

The sunshine picked up with a show of strength as they drove out on to the gravel road leading to the reservoir. *The* reservoir. Cowley knew it had to be the right one. If it was not – he would not contemplate that.

The C.I.5 man assigned here, Bill Biggs, had been keeping an alert look out. But he had seen nothing. He told Cowley so. They looked around. The water sparkled in that late burst of sunshine. The ski jumps stood out sharp in the water, distant. Trees bent over the water along one bank, the sheds bulked against the skyline on the other. Wildfowl chattered and squawked. A small hill lifted at their backs, brush-covered, silent, apparently deserted. It was very quiet, a quietness made all the more ominous by the metallic cries of the birds.

'A long shot,' said Cowley. 'And the wrong shot.'

He started to move back to the car. He limped with purpose.

Doyle said: 'The balloon doesn't go up until five thirty –'

'And it's just five now. No – that's long enough.'

'Just give us a chance to check the area,' said Bodie.

'We're talking about hundreds of thousands of lives!'

73

'Just a couple more minutes?' pleaded Doyle.

'A couple of lousy minutes,' said Bodie, truculently.

Then, before Cowley could argue, they turned and started off.

Charles Nesbit had worked everything out beautifully. His device attached to the target would explode at a predetermined time after he had set it off with a shot through the centre. He crouched by the bushes atop the little hill overlooking the reservoir where he had picked up silly Susan, water-skiing. His ultimatum had gone to the P.M. and although nothing had come in over the radio so far, there was still half an hour to go. His mind fastened with glee on his own cleverness. He had sent Sutton, who owed him favours in the line of obtaining drugs, to make sure Susan never talked. Now he had only to put a bullet into the target out there by the ski ramp and a gallon of A.D.X. would go beautifully bubbling into the reservoir. Let them try to cheat him on the deal – and that's what they'd get!

He edged out past the bush and saw that the stupid plainclothes policeman who had been there for some time had been joined by three other men. Well, they didn't think he was going to stand on the bank and pour the stuff in, did they? And then he giggled. Perhaps they did. Perhaps they had no idea at all.

He ran a hand over the Winchester. He'd seen off those men who'd come screeching up to his house. Now he'd see just how clever they were – he moved back into cover and his foot came down with a crunch on the transistor radio.

Even as he bent with a muffled cry to the radio he saw the two men below running up towards him. He could not know now if his demands had been met. His mind, obsessed with his own cleverness, confused, tortured by self-guilt for the world, blew. He knew he had been betrayed. They had come to his house and now they were coming for him – here!

Nesbit flopped down, lifted the Winchester, took a deliberate aim through the scope, quietening his hectic breathing,

74

fighting the tremble, hearing his heart thudding – and pressed the trigger.

He saw he had hit clean. But, to make sure, he loosed off two more Long Rifles. Now the device he had fixed up would explode and jettison a gallon of drugs into the water!

That was showing them!

His job done, Nesbit started to scramble away up the hill.

The shots blatted from the hillside, echoing out over the water, sending the flocks of wildfowl cawing into the air. Cowley and his men hit the scanty cover and came up on the alert, guns out, peering. They had seen no evidence of strikes. Doyle, quartering the ground upslope, saw the scrambling form of Nesbit take off. Instantly, Doyle was on his feet, chasing.

'There! Up there!' he bellowed.

Bodie roared up and then cut off at an angle. Biggs went pounding along after them. For a heartbeat Cowley waited transfixed, then he started after his men.

Doyle and Bodie were a team. Bodie and Doyle were professionals.

They sprinted upslope after Nesbit, came in at him from two sides. Doyle fired a warning shot into the air, bellowing to Nesbit to hold it. The hunted man whirled about, shaking, showing his teeth. He whipped the Winchester up into his shoulder, and Bodie, shooting from a perfect stance, blasted the rifle from Nesbit's grip. The whang of the nine-millimetre slug vibrated tingling all along Nesbit's arms, as though his rifle had suddenly become red hot. He yelled.

Biggs panted up. 'No one hurt?'

The handguns levelled on Nesbit, who stood, shuddering.

'No,' said Doyle. 'He wasn't shooting at us.'

'Then where, then?'

'I thought it went over me, out across the water . . . '

They pushed Nesbit back downslope as Cowley came into view. Once glance reassured him the situation was under control. He started in: 'Charles Nesbit. It's all over – '

At this Nesbit stopped his shuddering and realised once again just how clever he had been. 'All over? All over! It hasn't even started yet.'

Bodie dug out a pair of binoculars from the car and started to scan over the water where Biggs thought the shots had gone. He heard what Nesbit said. He didn't like the sound of it. He saw the ski ramp, panned on, then jerked back. A target – red, white and blue, just like the ones in the packet in Nesbit's cluttered room. 'That's what he was shooting at.'

Doyle was now peering through his glasses. 'More than that. Look lower . . .'

'You're too late,' said Nesbit, crowing, filled with his own importance. 'Too damned late.'

'There's a thing – some kind of thing, device, what-have-you, fitted below the target,' said Doyle.

Bodie nodded. 'It's a delayed fuse. Hit the target – set off the fuse – whammy –'

Doyle said: 'Sets it off when?'

'When this miserable creep's well away –'

'Which doesn't give us much time if I'm any judge.'

'No time at all,' said Cowley.

Bodie jumped into the boat Nesbit had used and took a grip of the outboard starting line. Doyle, with a quick confirming glance at Cowley, urged Nesbit down into the boat. Cowley sweated this one out. But he shouted just as the outboard broke into life: 'Our time's up!'

Bodie and Doyle exchanged a look compounded of wry amusement and downright grim bloody-mindedness.

Then Doyle said: 'Come in Number Twenty-seven . . .'

' . . . your time's up,' finished Bodie.

The boat sped across the water heading for the ski ramp. Nesbit, still handcuffed, felt bewilderment at the speedy turn of events.

Cowley ripped up the handset and within a very few moments was patched through the net to the P.M.'s office. He spoke vehemently. 'Sir? Cowley . . . Can you bear with me for sixty seconds? Just sixty seconds!'

The boat cut around and the engine died and Bodie was out and over the side. He ducked down. The target above water and the device below it topped a metal container. His experience told him a great deal of the nature of this deadly device and he felt around underwater for the fuse. The water was cold. On the surface Doyle looked over the side anxiously, and then quickly back to Nesbit. Bodie's head broke surface.

'Device all right – '

'You know, Bodie, if it blows – while we're still here?'

Bodie said: 'We won't know a thing.' Then he sucked a huge breath and ducked down again. The tension hung. Doyle lowered down on Nesbit, hating him for putting Bodie through this.

'You, Nesbit, might be martyred. Because if that thing goes up you go with it.'

Bodie popped into view again, whooping for breath.

'Some kind of linkage and a cap . . .'

This time he put his hands under water and reached around, feeling, feeling his way. 'It's stiff. If I can get some kind of purchase on it . . .'

Doyle leaned out of the boat alongside Bodie. The boat tipped dangerously. 'Another hand . . .'

After a bit, Doyle slid over the side and worked with Bodie in the water. They strained, trying to untwist the cap.

'Got . . . ?'

'Yeah . . . Go ahead . . . turn . . .'

'I – am . . .'

Then: 'It's moving!' Bodie yelped. 'I can feel it moving – '

Nesbit abruptly reared up rocking the boat. He shouted. His face looked ghastly, beaded with sweat, his eyes glaring.

'For God's sake – no!' At this the partners froze. 'There's an anti-handling device . . .'

Bodie and Doyle, their numbed hands gripping the cap, trod water and did not move the cap a millimetre.

'Dummy cap turns clockwise . . . Real one's beneath – anti-clockwise . . . '

Bodie and Doyle just looked. Then: 'You heard what the man said,' offered Bodie.

'Anti-clockwise.'

'Anti-clockwise.'

They started work again and now Nesbit, blue, shaking, shattered, called: 'Be careful. There's a trembler.'

Once more the partners gulped air.

'Trembler,' said Doyle.

'Trembler,' said Bodie.

'Busy little bastard, ain't he?'

They proceeded and they were extraordinarily careful. But their training held up. Nesbit collapsed on the bottom boards, curled up, blue, but no longer shivering. He was rigid with terror.

Abruptly Bodie let out a small, chopped off cry. Nesbit screamed and tried to fling himself across the boat, and tripped and fell. Bodie bobbed up with a wicked-looking fuse device in his hand. Casually, he tossed it into the air.

'Bodie! Don't *do* that!'

They heaved themselves back into the boat and looked down on the pseudo-idealist. He sprawled in the boat where he had fallen, jerking now, moaning and writhing, stricken.

Bodie said: 'Not with a bang – '

Doyle said: 'But with a whimper.'

They started the outboard and headed for shore where Cowley, watching, let loose a long, long sigh, and then, briskly, professionally spoke into the handset mike.

'Cowley, sir. You won't have to make that announcement after all.'

The boat created a most beautiful pattern of overlapping ripples in the water of the reservoir – in the undrugged water. When Nesbit was manhandled ashore and handed over to Biggs and seen off, Cowley regarded his two alleged top-agents reflectively. 'You did well.'

Bodie looked up. He felt damned cold. 'Careful, sir – we're

not accustomed to such adulation.' He was shivering now, shaking, and he couldn't stop it.

Cowley's hard, ruthless face bore down. His seamed skin and craggy appearance with those alert intelligent eyes boring through Bodie boded no good tidings for anyone, least of all operatives of the Action Squad, the Big A.

'Nerves, Bodie?'

'No – no.' Bodie tried to control his shaking jaws. 'That wa – water's damned cold!'

Cowley nodded. He straightened. 'Well, I have a wee nip of Scotch in the car that should cure that.'

Bodie beamed, the shivering already psychosomatically reducing under the ministrations of the Scotch to come. 'Thank you, sir.'

Cowley and Bodie moved towards the car.

Doyle frowned. He hurried after them, calling out, and starting to put on the most tremendous fit of the shakes.

'S – sir! I'm co – cold, too!'

Chapter Seven

Sir Charles Milvern presented the appearance of a large, well-fleshed, smooth man, with the controlled manners of gentle breeding adequately concealing the rough brown-bear core to him. The lights of his office reflected from his immaculately pomaded hair, grey-silver, sleek, smooth. Now he spoke smoothly into the telephone, glancing at his wrist watch as he spoke.

'Well, I'm not in the Government, you know. Not yet, anyway.'

From his expression it was perfectly clear Sir Charles Milvern was charming his listener.

'Still just shadow minister . . . "Not yet?" All right, you can quote me. And, I'll be more specific. In my opinion the electorate of this country will put us back into power within the next twelve months. Yes. You're welcome.'.

He thumbed the intercom and as he hung up, his secretary, a prim, prissy woman in a fawn twin-set, walked in. Sir Charles raise his eyebrows at her, and sighed, and said: 'I won't need my chauffeur any more today, Jessica. I'm going down to the country. Driving myself.'

'Yes, Sir Charles – you haven't forgotten that the Prime Minister –'

'No. No, I haven't forgotten. I'll contact him later.'

Milvern checked his office, picked up his brief case and left with a good afternoon to Jessica. He descended in the lift and nodded as the doorman touched his cap to him. The Bentley was ready, and the chauffeur, not displeased at the prospect of a night off, opened the door. Milvern liked the big Bentley; he drove rather well, he thought. The Prime Minister – well, later he would find out just what was hatching there . . .

He pulled out and eased towards the corner, ready to turn into the busy Victoria Street. He was looking forward to getting away from the cares – not of office, but of preparing for office – and he gave a shrug to his beefy shoulders in the Savile Row grey suit, smiling.

Across the street the Ford Capri in all-black parked with the near-side wheels on the kerb attracted no notice from Milvern; although the Yellow-Perils would be along at any moment. In the Capri Simon Culver saw Milvern in the big Bentley and gave the signal to Sara, who waited further along. Sara saw the signal and braced herself. This was going to be a bit scarey – but she was hooked into scarey things by now. Her blood tingled through her veins as she watched the Bentley advancing slowly to the corner.

Sara had been dressed very carefully by Culver. She looked bright and sexy, young and naïve with it, and yet Culver had managed the voluptuous attraction without making Sara look tarty. He prided himself on knowing about women. Now Sara, her young face expertly made-up, her high-heels tapping the pavement, walked towards the kerb. She carried a shopping basket packed with a supermarket's best. She glanced covertly at the Bentley under her eyelashes – Culver had forbidden her to wear false eyelashes, for her own were perfect. She judged the distance perfectly.

She stepped into the road.

Milvern saw the pretty girl step off the pavement and he slammed on the anchors, cursing. At the last minute, the girl stepped back, abandoning her shopping bag. Packets of cereal, cans of fruit, wrapped slices of pâté fragmented squashily under his wheels. The car stopped. Milvern let out an explosive grunt.

On the kerb Sara put her hands to her face. Although she had judged it well and the Bentley had not been travelling

6

fast enough for real danger, Sara could feel the dampness on her body.

Sir Charles jumped out, pushed through a crowd who were clearly hostile to him and his big car.

'Are you all right?'

Sara looked at him with those big blue eyes, and smiled.

Across the road the Capri started up and bumped into the road, moved slowly off skirting the Bentley. It had all worked out beautifully. Simon Culver tapped on the steering wheel in time to the cassette, and smiled. Very nice.

Ann Seaford returned to her flat in a most exclusive part of Kensington – well, almost the most exclusive, of course – to find Simon Culver looking very pleased with himself. He was going around the flat tidying up. By the telephone table he shuffled the books into order and pulled the jotter back into position. Sara had taken Sir Charles beautifully. The man had swallowed hook, line and sinker. He'd even rung to postpone some appointment or other. Sara had been changing into something just a wee bit – a teeny wee bit – more sexy at the time, pretending Ann Seaford's flat was her own.

'How did you make out?' asked Culver.

Ann smiled and opened her purse, took out a cheque. She waved it at Culver. He smiled back.

'He was generous – '

'He was a *louse*! I don't want to see him again, ever. Tell Wences.'

'Tell him yourself. He'll be picking me up here – '

'What are you doing here, anyway?' Ann's key was not her own.

'We used the flat for a little badger job.'

Ann wanted to wash the feel of that louse's hands off her. She stripped off her blouse and dropped it on the floor, and then her bra. She wriggled out of her skirt and then saw the two silver-framed photos standing on a side table. They were new. Ann Seaford looked ravishing. Had she not done so, she would not have been so successful. Around thirty-five, she possessed a figure to make a man's eyes pop out – although it was not his eyes she was after. It was the contents of his wallet. Now she saw the photo of Sara in the silver frame and her hands halted as they began to strip her panties off.

'She was the bait,' said Culver.

'This girl? Do you know who she is?'

Culver was wrapped in the success of his scheme. 'I know she has a great future. I picked her up at Paddington a couple of months ago.'

'She . . . ' Ann still had not moved. 'She looks very young.'

'Yeah, that was a problem. But I solved it – '

'In your usual way?'

'Surely. Got her hooked on to me – then the good life – then *really* hooked – now. She'll do anything for her daily fix.'

Ann began mechanically moving again, stripping off her panties, kicking them away. She felt strange. 'Get me a drink, will you?'

Simon pushed the photo into his side pocket. It only just slid in. 'Sure. The usual?'

He went back towards the other room and Ann looked about, as though dazed, not really with it. She shivered. She picked up the mink coat draped over the back of the chesterfield and closed the bathroom door, and looked back to where Culver was making ice-cube noises. Purposefully now, she moved to the door.

When Culver returned the room was empty. He shrugged and went to the bathroom door, knocked. No answer. He opened the door. He looked about again, realised the mink coat was gone, and started for the door. He pulled the door open and Wences was standing there, his finger reaching for the bell.

'Wences! Did Ann come past you?'

'No.'

Wences was a tall, slim Negro, superbly but unflashily

dressed, a man who knew about life and used that knowledge cleverly.

'She must have taken the back way. She just ran out –'

'What did you say to her?'

Wences moved into the apartment with an easy rhythm and Culver fussed along. 'Say? Nothing – ' He pulled the photo of Sara from his pocket. 'We were talking about this girl –'

Wences saw the picture. He grabbed it. '*This* girl! This the girl you're using on the badger job?' He was mad. 'Why the Hell didn't you show me?'

'Why the Hell should I? *I* found her –'

'And you found big trouble, too. Now we've got to find Ann – and fast!'

The houses passed in a blur as Ann sat crouched in the corner of the taxi. This was Battersea and she knew this area, this was where she'd started after running away from home, and having the trouble handled for her, and now she was back here and in trouble of a different kind. Her hand gripped her purse in the pocket of the mink – thank God she always kept a purse there to save keep on undoing her coat – and she watched as the old house came up, and passed, and she looked ahead again to the house where Ray Doyle lived. He'd help her – as he had before when he'd been – oh, well, Ray was a copper and so that settled that.

She rang the doorbell and the bespectacled man who opened was a stranger. He looked at her vaguely, holding the empty milk bottle, too late to have it collected. Ann's feet touched the full bottles on the stone step.

'Ray Doyle moved from here – oh, three years ago. Went across the river. Chelsea. Went up in the world.'

'Do you know where?'

'No – but I think I have his address – ' The man, Alan Reeves, wandered back to the hall table still clutching his milk bottle. Ann looked up and down the almost deserted street – and abruptly gasped. So they'd followed the taxi –

that big flashy Yank car was Wences's. It had to be. That was him and Simon – she looked at the man in the hallway fumbling in the drawer with old bits and pieces of paper – and she knew she had no time. She turned and ran down the street, heading for the river. Alan Reeve suddenly pounced with a cry of triumph and came up with a scrap of paper.

When he reached the open door the girl in the mink coat was gone. A big American car abruptly squealed its tyres in a dramatic turn, just like American movies, and revved up going down the street. Reeves stared, puzzled, and saw the mink-coated girl turn into a side street leading to the river. The car followed.

He shook his head and went back inside. She had looked a nice girl – bit hard about the eyes and mouth – but nice . . .

Simon Culver jumped out of the car as Wences slewed it in front of the now running Ann. The side street was deserted. She halted, her hand gripping the mink coat to her throat, her face distraught.

'Ann,' said Culver in his smooth voice. 'Ann – what are you doing here?'

'I – I just needed a walk – get some air –'

'That's healthy. I approve.' Simon nodded. 'Well, don't let us stop you.'

For a moment Ann hesitated. Did these two mean what Culver said? She gripped the coat and tried to find a smile and walked past. As she passed him Culver reached out. He gripped the mink coat. He took a hefty handful into his hand. And he yanked.

The mink flew away from Ann.

She whirled, gasping.

Culver smirked. 'I'll accept you needed some air, Ann. But not *that* much air!'

Shaking, trembling, completely naked, Ann watched them. She tried to turn and run; but they were too quick. They closed in on her.

*

85

Ray Doyle's apartment had been tastefully decorated and furnished by an admirer – a lady interior decorator who had been great fun while she lasted – but Doyle had soon changed things around to suit himself. The pad looked more untidy than not untidy, and the presence of Bodie sprawled over a sofa getting to grips with Mary added a further note of untidiness. Both men wore evening dress, although it had clearly been through a night of some liveliness. Doyle let go of Sandra and padded across to fix the record player, which his admiring decorator friend had thought exciting to stuff into what had once been the fireplace.

Bodie took his lips away from Mary's – a charming girl, charming, whose evening dress slithered most gracefully from a shoulder that Bodie knew was rounded and creamy and everything else a voluptuous young lady's shoulder should be.

'That,' opined Bodie, 'was some speech the old man made.'

'A filibuster,' said Doyle flicking the on switch at last.

'D'you think he noticed we slipped away?'

'Probably,' said Doyle, going back to Sandra – who was, in his opinion, far more of a doll than Mary. 'Probably still talking.'

They had had a busy night. The drapes were drawn, soft rose-coloured lights glowed from the walls; but the night was long fled.

The telephone rang.

No one took any notice.

Presently, holding Mary very close and dancing casually, Bodie circled around the phone and shied a cushion over it. It went on ringing maddeningly.

Doyle took his hand away from Sandra and sat up. 'Could be important.'

Bodie, his hand now freed from the cushion, pulled Mary to him. 'More important than this? Anyway, we're off duty.'

'You're right. Absolutely right. Definitely.' He looked at the cushion. Sandra giggled and tickled his ear. 'But, on the other hand, you could be wrong.' Doyle dived for the phone, knocking the cushion away, letting Sandra flop back, laughing, and answered.

Bodie could make nothing of the call – a man called Reeves and a girl in a mink coat – Doyle cocked a hard eye at Mary who was trying with Bodie's mischievous assistance to do something dire to his hair – and so Bodie danced Mary away and let Doyle get on with the call.

When he hung up Doyle moved thoughtfully to the window, almost unconsciously avoiding Sandra who tried to embrace him, and flung back the drapes. Daylight broke in, making Bodie wince.

A little miffed, Sandra said: 'Ray?'

Bodie knew a fair amount about Ray Doyle by now. They were partners. He gave Mary a pat on that delectably-rounded bottom and said: 'Why don't you two girls go and make some coffee?'

When the girls, who saw by Bodie's smile that something was in the wind, had gone, Bodie sat up, pushing: 'What happened to the party spirit?'

'A woman just turned up at the place I used to live. Very upset – asking for me –'

Bodie said: 'And ever so slightly pregnant?'

Doyle regarded him dispassionately. 'When I was on the Drug Squad maybe a dozen contacts had my address. And strict instructions not to use it unless it was very, very important.'

'Doyle – that has to be three years ago, at least.'

'Yes.' Doyle stared out the window. 'Someone was chasing her.'

Bodie recognised the symptoms. Well, hell, he was Ray Doyle's partner, wasn't he. 'Okay,' said Bodie.

Doyle turned. 'Okay, what?'

'Okay, we'll go and check. That's what you want, isn't it?'

Doubtfully, Doyle said: 'The girls – ?'

'Leave 'em to me.'

Doyle went to fetch his car and by the time he was out front on a morning that promised some sunshine Bodie was

87

waiting. As they drove off heading for Battersea, Doyle asked what Bodie had told the girls to get them off the hook.

'That we,' said Bodie, sitting back in the passenger seat and relaxing, 'had turned gay and are running off to get married.' He looked thoughtful. 'Of course they knew it wasn't true. I wouldn't marry you if you were the last man on Earth.'

Doyle turned the wheel and headed past traffic, overtaking.

'You're right. I'm much too good for you.'

Reeves's information sent them along the side street that led to the river. They stopped and got out, and then looked about, up and down. A few people hurried past. The smell of the river lifted, not too unpleasant, tangy. A tug with a line of lighters went chugging past. 'Any idea who she might have been?' said Bodie.

Doyle nodded. 'Sounds like Ann Seaford. A tall blonde – mind you, she could be a brunette or a redhead now –'

Bodie walked to the embankment and looked up and down the river. The early sun flung coins of silvered gold back at him from the water. He stopped moving and looked down. His shoulders went rigid. When he spoke his voice was flat.

'This Ann Seaford. Was her hair long – down to her shoulders?'

Doyle turned and walked quickly to join Bodie at the embankment wall, and looked down, into the water, past a jumble of floating debris.

Ann Seaford floated there, naked, her long blonde hair flowing out in the water. Her body looked very white indeed against the oily green.

When the ambulance had been called and the girl's lifeless body had been taken away, Bodie looked at Doyle, and then said in a matter-of-fact tone: 'Suicide.'

'Yeah?' Doyle sounded suddenly fierce. 'Then why haven't we found the mink coat? What did she do with the fur coat?'

They walked back to the car jerkily. Bodie said: 'She

tossed it down before she jumped. Some joker picked it up and – '

'Maybe. And what about the men chasing her?' He started up. 'Big flash car. A black gentleman. Add 'em together and what do you get? A pimp is what you get. A high class pimp for a high class hooker – and that's what Ann Seaford was!' The car started and meshed with the traffic. 'And judging from her latest address – still high class.'

The Kensington apartment confirmed that. The partners went up in the lift, conscious of the refined air of elegance. A highly swish residence, indeed. As Bodie said: 'High class, indeed! Who did she hook – Croesus?'

Doyle's comment paid a kind of tribute to Ann Seaford. 'If he was a man – it's very likely.'

'It's just suicide, Doyle. Not even our business.' They walked along the corridor to Ann's apartment door. 'Cowley'll eat you alive.'

Doyle paused, considering the implications. Then he said: 'Yeah!' and kicked the door in.

George Cowley took the lift up in this plush apartment block and went limping purposefully down the corridor to Ann Seaford's flat. A bulky, rubicund plain clothes man stood by the door, looking sourly out upon the world, his colour deceptive.

'Mr Cowley . . . ?'

'Well?'

'Detective Superintendent Tilson, sir. I called you – I had to. Those two boys of yours, sir, running rough-shod over my men. This is a probable suicide – possibly murder, though – and right out of C.I.5's jurisdiction – '

'*Nothing*,' said Cowley, acidly, 'is outside of C.I.5's jurisdiction.' He wasted no more words and pushed on through.

Inside, two police plain clothes men were scurrying around as Bodie and Doyle searched the apartment. One was just upending various papers on to the table carrying the telephone when Cowley entered. He glared. 'Doyle! Bodie!'

Then, to the policemen: 'Wait outside.' To his agents, he said: 'As far as I can see – a call girl who drowned herself.'

Doyle took a breath. 'This is personal, sir.'

'*Nothing* is personal, Doyle. When you joined C.I.5 I thought I made that perfectly clear. The department owns you. I can sell your body to science if I want – while it's still alive!'

Feeling for Doyle, Bodie interposed placatingly: 'We *are* off duty, sir –'

'Second mistake. And, yes, you did disappear sharpish last night . . . You're never off duty. That is one thing we do share with the police – and the only thing. Now I find you sharing a common suicide with them.'

'I knew her –' began Doyle.

'That's no answer. You're C.I.5, both of you – C.I.5 *special* assignments only –'

Doyle whipped out his ID as though popping his hand-gun. He waved it. 'With authority to investigate *any* and *every* incident. That's in the small print –'

'Don't quote small print at me! For every sentence of small print, I can produce smaller!' George Cowley was bombing along now, beautifully steamed up, giving them a real ripe roasting. 'This is a police matter. Leave it to the police.' He stared at them, fuming, and then turned to go, and that damned bad leg jinxed him and he lurched into the telephone table. Cowley grabbed for support, straightened, came up with the telephone jotter in his hand. Quite automatically, he stared at it.

The creases in that craggy face abruptly deepened. He whirled, limped to the door, bellowed.

'Superintendent Tilson!'

Tilson popped in, just wiping the huge grin of enjoyment off his face. He'd sicced this Cowley on to these C.I.5 boys and they'd had a right rollicking. 'Yes, sir?'

'I want this apartment sealed off. Clear your people out. We'll send in our own forensics men. This is now a C.I.5 case.'

90

'But – but –'

'Don't but me. D'you want to see the small print on our authority!'

Bodie and Doyle hung on to their chins as Cowley slammed the door after the undignified departure of Tilson. He turned back glaring at them. He lifted the telephone jotter.

'This phone number. Someone's been on the phone, calling this number, doodled it down. This number – it is the Prime Minister's private line!'

Intensive work was called for. Cowley began a run down on those few people who knew the P.M.'s private telephone number. The offices of C.I.5, drab, Spartan, functional, burst into that special kind of activity that peaked when an investigation began to open out to horizons leading on enticingly.

Cowley, rubbing that damned bad leg of his, grumbled. 'This is a lousy one.'

'Lousier than you think,' said Doyle. 'I reckon she was murdered.'

The facts on Ann Seaford as far as they were known were studied. Doyle insisted that, despite all, she'd been okay; as he said: 'She had a code of her own. Bent as you like, as long as you could pay. But if it came to something really bad, she was as straight as a die.'

Although Ann had run it alone when Doyle knew her, they assumed she must have turned to a protector now. She would need someone to cling to, as she grew older, security –

'I want him,' said Cowley. 'That pimp.'

Going out, Bodie said to Doyle, 'How do we do that?'

Doyle did not laugh as he said: 'How about being a customer?'

'I,' said Bodie, 'haven't paid for it since I was six years old. Cost me a whole bag of jelly babies.'

'You did start young. That why you're so good at it?'

'I'm not good at it. I just practise a lot.'

Chapter Eight

While Sir Charles Milvern found it incredible that anything like this could happen to him, he realised with a deliciously luxurious tremble that he was fully prepared to take advantage of the situation and to enjoy it right up to the hilt. This Sara – what a gorgeous dolly-bird she was! After their first accidental encounter she had taken to him in a very big way, bringing him back to her Uncle Sam's house, making him feel at home.

The house was grand, luxurious, tastefully furnished, highly sophisticated – and empty.

The overhead lighting flickered and reflected from the heated indoor swimming pool. Sara, swathed in a robe, came in and turned, beckoning Sir Charles on with a quick laughing:

'Now you have a swimming costume, Charles – naughty Charles to forget – we can swim no end. I'm all ready for it.'

She threw off the robe. Milvern caught his breath. She was slim, slender with youth, yet shaped, shaped breathtakingly. Her minute bikini looked as though it would blow away. She smiled and drew herself up, took a breath, and dived in. Charles Milvern followed eagerly. They surfaced together, and as the splashes cascaded out, Sara laughed shrilly.

They trod water and Sara readjusted her bikini top.

'Charley – you're so *naughty*!'

The swim proved highly pleasurable and then they climbed out, donned their robes and spread out in the chairs by the round metal table. Brandy was to hand. Sara lifted the glass Milvern filled for her and looked at him swimmingly over the rim.

'To us!'

Milvern lifted his glass. 'Serendipity.'

'Seren – what?'

'A happy accident.' They drank and then Sara leaned back and wiggled her toes, and then wiggled her body deliciously. 'Your uncle – ?' said Milvern, questioningly. 'Mr Baker – ?'

'Yes, this is Uncle Sam's house but he's away all day. We have the place to ourselves. Do you know what I usually do now? After a swim, while my body's still tingling and so alive? I usually go and lie on the bed.' They regarded each other and the lightning of understanding flashed. 'I'm a creature of habit.'

Softly, Milvern said: 'Some habits are good. Shouldn't be broken.'

Sara stood up, smiling. 'First on the right up the stairs. You go on – I'll bring some nice drinkeys.'

With a smile he tried not to make fatuous, Milvern went out and into the ornate hall and up the panelled stairs. Sara went through to the front quarters of the house.

She went into a room with a window opening on to the front gardens, where greenery glowed in the late sun.

Sam Baker waited for her, sitting in his leather armchair, rising as she entered – but rising not out of courtesy. Baker was around forty-five, tough, a teddy-bear of a man, packed with muscle, dominating his surroundings. He knew exactly what he wanted, and this little chit was one of the keys. That idiot Simon Culver had nearly fouled up with Ann Seaford; but Baker was assured that her death would look like suicide. Now he said to Sara: 'Well? The swimming costume okay?'

'Yes – Uncle Sam. He's going upstairs now.' Her eyes flicked towards a heavy bureau against the wall. 'Uncle Sam. Just one little sniff. I need it. I need it bad. If you want me to go through with this – ?'

Baker nodded. He opened the bureau and took out a cocaine sniffer. He had barely turned when Sara snatched it eagerly, her tense body slackening and loosening as she used the sniffer.

'Just one,' said Baker, firmly. 'But more – much more later – after you've done your job.' He patted her bottom. 'Now go and – entertain – him, my dear.'

When Sara had wiggled her way out, Baker picked up a microphone from the study desk and said: 'Culver?'

The speaker alongside crackled and Culver's voice answered.

'They're on their way up,' Baker told him.

'I'm ready.'

Sam Baker walked back to his big leather armchair and let himself down with a satisfied grunt. Things were panning out fine, just fine. His contacts would be pleased – and show their appreciation accordingly.

Night fell over the metropolis and the fairyland of lights switched on, driving away the night. In that part of London where the lights glittered the brightest there were to be found paradoxically those haunts where the lights did not reach, pools of shadow, infested by people whose day began when the lights outside switched on, emphasising their shadows. Bodie waited in the car by the kerb as Doyle crossed the pavement from the late-night tobacconists. He was tossing a packet of cigarettes in his hand and as he entered the car Bodie caught them. He looked and then sniffed.

'Scented cigarettes! You turning into a poofter, Doyle? And, anyway, you don't smoke.'

'We have to find this pimp, right?' Doyle took the packet back. 'Know thy subject. And the subject is a girl who will I hope lead me on the right way – I'll let you know.'

Bodie grunted and got out of the car. 'I'll be in the office turning out more dope. Keep in contact.'

'Now body contact is the name of the game – around here.'

The lights switched on in Sam Baker's luxurious house one by one as Sara led Milvern, laughing, from the front door through to the lounge. They burst in, laughing after a fabulous dinner, with Milvern saying: 'What about a moonlight dip? What about –'

He stopped dead. In the lounge, grouped, waiting, dark against the lights, three men turned their heads to survey him. He felt odd. The unexpected presence of men in what he had thought an empty house disoriented him. Sara was carrying a big fluffy teddy bear Milvern had bought her – symbol, really, of the kind of relationship he had thought they were building.

Now Sara contemptuously tossed the teddy bear away. She went to stand by Simon Culver, who took her arm, just above the elbow.

Baker took a step forward. He looked expressionlessly at Sir Charles Milvern. 'Sir Charles –'

Culver started to lead Sara away. She went gratefully. She threw a last look over her shoulder. 'Goodbye, Charley –'

Milvern shook, suddenly. He put out an unsteady hand.

Baker went on, remorselessly, now, as Culver and Sara left the lounge. 'Sir Charles, you have been taking a great interest in Sara. We, in turn, have been taking a great interest in you.'

Milvern just stood, hand half-raised, staring. Baker moved to the light switch. The third man, heavily-built, dark, about forty-five, with a compressed, powerful, brooding presence about him, moved to his side revealing a movie projector set up ready to operate. The screen against the far wall showed beaded white – and then Baker flicked the lights off.

The flickering images leaped from the cine projector, luminous ghosts began to writhe on the screen.

After a bracing encounter in a night club Doyle came up with the name of a girl who – it was said in that hinted-at, half-spoken, whispered way of these people – was run by the same protector as Ann Seaford. Doyle called out on the handset and arranged to meet Bodie at the address. Then he made another call, and came up with nothing from records. He made a face.

'All right,' he said, turning the car into the discreet apartment block – he seemed to be doing nothing but deal with apartment blocks lately, and that, of course, was fitting – 'Okay. If Murray says the pimp stays in, then the pimp stays in. If Murray says so. All right. Yes, Bodie's there.'

Bodie took a taxi and when Doyle arrived leaned in at the window. 'How will you play it, Doyle?'

Doyle pulled his S&W and handed it to Bodie. 'Drunk!'

Bodie watched as his partner entered the apartment block.

He shook his head. Doyle spent his formative years hanging out around hookers and pimps and the like, and Bodie fancied that was a sight more intriguing than humping a pack and a rifle and slogging over muddy miles – as he had done.

Doyle put on a convincing drunk act – not comic, just the right amount of slur in the voice, the exact meticulousness of movement, of over-compensation – and the girl, Jo, looked at him impatiently. Wences had called and now he waited in the other room and Jo wanted to get this pigeon dry and out of it.

Doyle smiled sloppily. 'You're not as pretty as she told me. Not nearly as pretty.'

Jo forced a smile, reminding herself the customer is always right. 'What I lack in looks I make up for in experience.'

'Yeah? How about a drink, then? A little drink?'

He reached for the whisky bottle on the tatty sideboard and Jo whisked it away. She still smiled; but the smile was edged-steel. 'Shouldn't we talk terms first?'

'Sure. Terms.' Doyle staggered and recovered. 'But not first.' The stagger brought him artistically near her and he grabbed the bottle. 'Drink first!'

He upended the bottle. Jo regarded him, pulling her flowered wrap closer to her. She felt unsure. But there was Wences in the next room. That was a comfort.

Doyle kept the tension up for as long as he felt he could

hold out, trying to manoeuvre the girl. He dared not allow any feeling for her into his calculations. The death of Ann Seaford was murder – it smelled of murder. And with that secret telephone number added in, feelings for one poor little tramp just did not fit.

Finally, Jo said, with more of an edge to her voice than good customer relations warranted: 'Terms!'

'Terms! I'm solvent.' Doyle lurched and then dragged out a ridiculous fancy credit card wallet, like a snake, packed with the coloured rectangles of plastic that passed as money in these enlightened times. 'Take your pick.'

Jo's face set. A flush stained along her cheekbones.

'No credit, mister. Strictly cash. Time is money – so – '

Doyle had to put pressure on. He sneered. It was a work of art, that sneer, with the curled nostril and the sliding lip. 'Truth is, I don't fancy you.' He swigged from the bottle again, as an angle so some ran down his chin. 'Your drink's all right – but you? How will you recoup? Report me to the Tourist Board?'

A voice, a voice honey-smooth, from the inner door, said: 'Take it out of your hide.' Wences appeared. His tall elegant form towered blackly in the room. The brass knucks glittered. 'And when your hide's all used up we'll take it out of your pockets.' He advanced menacingly. 'I'm throwing you out – *eventually.*'

The brass knucks glittered again as Wences swung a meaty punch that would have driven Doyle' belly-button through his spine. Doyle's fake drunkenness snapped off. He slid the blow and stepped to the side, took the brass knuckled fist with one hand and twisted it back. With his other hand he slammed a flat palm up under Wences's chin. He slammed him back. He slammed him back against the wall by the door. Wences's head thudded into the fancy wallpaper, and Doyle's palm went on with the blow, crunching under Wences's chin.

For a weird instant Wences's head vibrated like the clapper of a bell. Then Doyle gripped a fist into that fancy frilled shirt and hoisted the tall man up. Wences hung, almost out cold, and not a drop of blood anywhere.

Doyle started to urge Wences to the door. Half-way there he looked back at Jo. She stood, gripping her robe to her, her mouth open, her eyes – well, Doyle could allow emotion into himself, now and so he didn't look into her eyes.

He said: 'I lied. You're pretty. But the drink was lousy.'

Then he manhandled Wences out.

Simon Culver drove the all-black Capri fast. Sara was a curvaceous chick but she was fraying his nerves. She fidgeted and wouldn't keep still. She kept swallowing. He knew what the matter with her was and so he said to soothe her: 'Wences will have stuff.'

'That Charley,' said Sara. 'His hands – warm and soft, like a woman – ' She jittered, swinging from one mood to another. 'I need that stuff. I need it now!'

'Wences's place coming up, Sara. Take it easy – Hold it!'

The all-black Capri pulled into the kerb before Wences's apartment block. Doyle appeared manhandling the tall Wences and making for a car parked by the kerb. The man in the car looked across, and then back, and then got out to help stow Wences into the back seat, and then he got in beside him.

Stunned, Culver and Sara watched. Abruptly, Culver gunned the Capri away. He tried to stop the shakes. Sara felt the pangs of need and she raked forward, snapped open the glove compartment. If Wences was pinched . . .

The glove compartment yielded a variety of interesting objects; but none was remotely like what Sara craved.

'You know I don't carry in the car, Sara.'

'And you know I need my stuff – Simon, you promised me – '

'When we get to my place. We have to see Baker first – Wences – Hell! What'll Baker say?'

Sara's blue eyes showed a flicker of cunning intelligence. She sat back, smiling. 'Uncle Sam. Uncle Sam always keeps stuff.'

The battered old desk lamp shone down on Cowley's desk and the pile of stuff his agents had picked up from Ann Seaford's flat. A lot more was being sifted in forensics; but he felt he was getting nowhere, fast. His secretary walked across with a worn envelope that looked as though it had been opened and closed many times. 'There's this, sir.'

Cowley shook out a dozen photos, black and whites, and, as the subject, the same girl in each, grew older, coloured. He frowned. They were a pathetic record of a child growing up – pathetic, Cowley knew at once with that sense of his, and Betty supplied the rationalisation to that fey feeling.

'They were hidden away, sir, with this.' She placed a curl of hair on the photos. The hair was tied with pink ribbon. 'A baby's curl.'

Cowley looked tartly at Betty. 'You checked – ?'

Betty showed him a faded, rumpled letter in which the curl of hair had been kept. The letter was dated eighteen years ago. It read: Dear Miss Seaford, You must understand that it would be quite impossible for you to see your daughter now or at any time. We are now her legal parents. She is our child now.'

Cowley shook his head and riffled through the photos. The letter finished: 'You will appreciate that in view of your life style there can be no question of you ever meeting your daughter. However, we are quite willing to send you photographs of her from time to time. By the way, we have decided to call her Sara.'

The last photo showed the girl was turning into a beautiful woman; but she was still young – the letter date made her eighteen or so. The door opened and Cowley looked up, ready to blast any intruder.

He saw a tall, slim black man impeccably dressed but who looked a little the worse for wear. He reeled into the office, and then halted, as though worked with wires. Bodie and Doyle stepped in. They smiled.

Cowley said, 'The pimp?'

'The pimp. He's in, like Murray said.'

'Henry Aloysius Wences. Take a seat, Aloysius,' said Bodie. 'A sixteenth-century popular Spanish saint, Aloysius,' said Bodie, who was a fount of this kind of information. 'You're very popular around here.'

Wences sat down and glared around, still elegant but showing signs of incipient nervousness.

'This is not a regular bust. You're not coppers!'

'No,' Cowley told him. 'We're much worse. Tell me about Ann Seaford.'

'I never heard of her.'

'You would know all about them, of course, in your capacity as – ah – technical adviser?'

'Look – I know my rights. I've been busted before – ' He half rose and Doyle shoved him back. 'To hold me you've got to charge me – with what? Something to do with Ann Seaford – ' He started to shout. 'Well, I've told you I don't know her, and you've got to prove different. And you can't – you can't make out any link between us.'

His outburst brought him to his feet and moving forward as Cowley said: 'Ann Seaford – ' Wences broke forward and Doyle stepped in again to grab him.

Doyle gripped his arm to swing him about and plonk him back in the chair, and Wences abruptly stiffened. His face which had been filled with expression, annoyed, half-scared, building an anger, smoothed into an impassive black mask. The lights sheened across the dark skin, catching a bead of sweat, shadowing the hollows. But he had been slow. He was a professional but he'd been slow.

Cowley was on to it like a sailor at a bung hole.

He tapped the photos of Sara.

'Yes, Mr Wences? Know this girl, do you – ?'

'No.' Wences was still more shaken than he showed. 'No – '

'Oh, yes,' said Cowley, and now his voice grated like sandpaper. 'Oh, yes you do.' He took the latest picture of Sara and shoved it under Wences's nose. 'You know her.'

Bodie leaned across, looking hard at the photo.

'Well, if he doesn't – I certainly do.'

Bodie took the photo and studied it; but he was confident.

'Saw her less than half an hour ago – in a car – all-black Capri – ' He swivelled and glared at Wences. 'Right outside your place.'

Wences slumped back into the chair, helped by Doyle's hand. He maintained his poise; but all three Big A men could see he had been shaken. Cowley went on pouring it on.

'Now isn't that a coincidence, Mr Wences.'

Wences began to break up. They could see the process beginning. 'I want a lawyer. I'm saying nothing until I've seen a lawyer.'

The process was beginning; but it would take time, too much time.

'Saying nothing?' said Cowley in a mild voice of surprise and reproof. 'We'll see.' He glanced up at his two agents. 'Interrogation room – '

Bodie hefted Wences to his feet. The tall man babbled wildly, swinging his arms. 'This isn't legal – you have to charge me – it isn't legal – '

Reflectively, Bodie said: 'A few gut-sinkers . . . '

In the same mournful tone, Doyle added: 'And a few wrist-wrenchers . . . '

'I'll tell you something, Wences,' said Bodie. 'It may not be legal in one sense – it isn't even going to be fun – '

'You see, Mr Wences,' cut in Cowley. 'There are different levels of morality. We play by the book, strictly by the book – but the book is written by different people from those who wrote the book you wish to quote from. A murder has been committed with ramifications of which – we think – you are fully aware. We wish to know what those ramifications are.' To Bodie, harshly, he snapped, 'Take him away!'

Doyle lingered a moment, flicking his gaze to the scattered photos.

'Who is she, anyway – the girl?'

Cowley gave it to him straight. 'Ann Seaford's daughter.'

Chapter Nine

The projector in Baker's lounge whirred away to silence. The pictures on the screen died. The pictures – Sir Charles Milvern sat with his head cradled in his hands, his fingers clasped over that elegant grey-silver hair style. He had never imagined – they must have processed the films themselves, very quickly, and they were clever, very clever.

Baker remained impassive as he said: 'Inventive and physically very impressive. But, I think we can agree, Sir Charles, not the stuff that votes are made of?'

Milvern did not reply. Baker looked across at the hard, compact, powerful man in the sober suit with the bulge under the left armpit. 'He needs a drink – yes, perhaps he needs a drink.'

No one moved towards the drinks cabinet. Milvern lifted his head. His face was drawn, haggard. He looked ten years older. 'What do you want?' Silence. 'How much?'

Baker put his fingertips together. 'Difficult to measure, Sir Charles. The total destruction of a political career? A shattered marriage? And the laughter . . . Yes, perhaps, worst of all, the laughter, the disdain. Difficult to measure in terms of money.' He turned away, judging his words. 'So we will not bother with it.'

Milvern sat hunched, staring up, the agony and the disgust struggling with puzzlement. His hands shook.

'Let us just say,' went on Baker. 'A service rendered. You are in a privileged position, Sir Charles.' He smiled, a smile that transfixed Milvern. 'We would like to share that privilege.'

The agony and the despair and the distraught feelings of the ending – 'Share?' said Sir Charles Milvern. For the first time the dark, compact man spoke. His voice carried the faintest inflexion, a trill to the Rs, a meticulousness to the English accents, that marked him as unEnglish.

'There is a file on the economic and industrial disposition of Europe in the event of war.' He continued to speak as Sir Charles shifted, trying to interrupt. 'We know it exists. We know that it has a high security classification. We know that you, as Shadow Minister, have access to it.'

Milvern thought that the horror had been overwhelming up to then; it was then he realised the horror was only just beginning. There was no way he could argue, nothing he could do against these men – these shadowy men who had used a young girl to their own vile ends. Broken, Milvern was at last allowed to leave when the details had been arranged. Sam Baker returned from seeing the shattered Milvern off and, now, he did pour two drinks.

'Well,' he said, turning with the drinks in his hand. 'You will get your file.'

The answer of this dark and dangerous man astonished Baker, who was in it for the money. 'The file! I read the entire contents of it three months ago in Moscow!'

Baker's hand grasping his drink shook, suddenly. This sombre, enigmatic, brooding man went on with a vengeful rich satisfaction oozing from every word.

'It is not the file I want. It is *him* – for the rest of his natural life! The minute he commits that act of betrayal he belongs to me. A respected politician who will one day figure in the Government – in *my* pocket. I think I will take that drink now.'

Wordlessly, for all his own harsh toughness uncomfortably impressed by the latent violence in this man, Baker handed the drink across.

The arrival of Simon Culver, breathless, flustered, brought in a strange way, for all his news, a reduction in Baker's tenseness. He ushered Culver into the lounge and the three men tried to see around this latest development.

'Wences has been arrested,' said Baker, to be interrupted again by Culver speaking in a flurried, breathless way.

'Listen, we don't know *why* he was pulled in. Wences *gets* busted every now and then – he's in that kind of business.'

'But,' said the foreign man with the harsh voice. 'We don't know why.'

'What's it matter?' said Simon Culver. 'Wences won't talk.'

'And if he did,' pointed out Baker, 'what could he tell them? He knows none of the details of this affair. He doesn't even know that you or I exist.'

The dark man spoke directly to Culver. 'He could lead them to you.'

'And where would that get them?'

'One step closer to me,' the dark man said.

Culver flicked his eyes across. It was suddenly hot in the lounge.

'But that's ridiculous! You don't think *I* would talk, do you?' Culver showed the nervousness appearing on his face. He shook his head, quickly. 'You don't honestly think that, do you? Look, I'm in this up to my neck. I killed Ann for you! And Sara – who found Sara?'

'Yes,' said the foreigner in his faintly accented voice. 'Where is Sara?'

'Why – waiting outside in the car.'

That was where Sara had been left by Culver, as he had told her, for only a minute or two, sweetie, until he'd told Baker the news about Wences. But Sara wanted her fix. She climbed out of the car and walked up the drive and then, remembering, her eyes went to the window of the study fronting the garden. No lights showed. She lifted her hand to ring the front door bell, and then hesitated, knowing how mad Baker would be. She looked again at the open window of the study. She went quietly across and looked in. The bureau stood against the wall. She knew what Baker – he had fixed up for her to call him Uncle Sam for the sake of that

Charley – she knew damn well what Baker kept in that bureau.

Making up her mind, dry as all hell, she climbed in the window.

The bureau opened soundlessly. Where did he keep it? In that little drawer . . . She opened it, holding her breath; it made no sound. Frantically she rummaged around. She did not find what she so eagerly sought. There was not even a coke sniffer. She began to throw things out wildly, the hum of men's voices from the lounge no distraction.

Simon Culver took a step back at the dark secretive violence in this hard man. Baker was aware that all the tension had returned, that a cloud of breaking terror existed and would burst about them at any moment.

'I now have Sir Charles Milvern in my pocket. My own man within the Establishment. And the greatest advantage of all is that no one knows who he is outside Mr Baker and myself.' The dark, seamed face with the thick lips turned to regard Culver. 'Except you and Sara, of course.'

Culver moved back, chilled by the matter-of-fact way the words were spoken, realising too late what they meant. He tried to make a run for it, and big hands clasped around his neck. He was dragged around bodily, his feet lifting from the deep-pile carpet. A flailing hand caught the bottle display and cascaded a shining avalanche of bottles and glasses to the floor. Baker stood back. This was a high policy decision – and, anyway, it made sense.

Those thick powerful hands clamped Culver's neck. They choked. They gripped. They worked together, tighter and tighter. Culver's eyes started out, protruding, his tongue jammed between his teeth. He was trying to choke and making awful tearing sounds, spluttering, gagging, gurgling away to silence. He was thrown down. Knees slammed into him, the hands constricted tightly and more tightly. Culver's heels drummed maniacally upon the soft carpet. Drummed, and a long shuddering shiver went through his body, and he lay still. Still those hands clamped his neck. Still the ridged thumbs pressed in. Only when he was lax and still past the time a normal man might hold his breath was his throat released.

The big dark man stood up, stepped away, breathing deeply. He flexed his shoulders. Baker moved forward and looked down.

In the study Sara knew, with a hopeless feeling, that there was nothing here. She glared around and heard harsh words from the lounge, consciously identifying them for the first time. Her eyes darted about. A terrible – a horrible – gasping wheezing choking sounded. Then there was a heavy thump, like a body falling. Then she heard Baker – Uncle Sam – say: 'He's dead.'

Sara felt the enormous thump through her. She turned and knocked against the cut-glass ashtray. The thing skidded, toppled for an agonising instant on the desk edge, and then fell against the metal waste-paper basket.

In the lounge Baker stepped back from Culver's body.

The lights glowed mellowly. The room looked normal. But a corpse sprawled on the floor with a bitten-through tongue and glazed eyes, the black bruise marks beginning to show on the ruptured neck.

'I'll send in a team to wipe clean, Baker. First – we have to kill the girl.'

A slight clatter, almost unheard, from the study brought both men around. Before Baker could move his companion broke for the study door. He kicked the door in. With a single comprehensive glance he saw the rifled bureau, the fallen ashtray, the open window against which the curtains still fluttered.

'The girl!' he shouted. Then: 'The car! Culver's car!'

Both men ran out of the study and out of the house on to the drive. They belted down. The all-black Capri started up with a wildly over-revved engine, shot away with a lurching roar, burning rubber. The dark foreigner had to fling himself out of the way. He and Baker stared furiously after Sara as she drove away like a soul tormented – as, indeed, Baker instantly knew she was.

They went back to the house. 'What was she looking for, Baker?'

'Coke. Cocaine.'

'Did she find it?'

'No. Once the job was done I disposed of all – '

'She didn't find it,' the foreigner said, hard, compact, the suppressed violence in him now once again, as it had with Culver, preparing to burst out like a volcano. 'So she still needs it. Where? She knows no one else in the city – where will she go?'

Baker nodded towards the lounge. Culver's legs were just visible, sprawled laxly, his highly-polished shoes gleaming.

'Culver's place.'

George Cowley had formed C.I.5 to combat domestic crime, with an assignment from the Home Office that allowed him great latitude in his directives. His expertise and the peculiar talents of the men he had recruited yielded startling results. As he leaned forward and snapped off the desk lamp, for the new day was at hand, he reflected that there was no peace for the would-be-virtuous besides the wicked.

He sat back in the old office chair and put the forefinger and thumb of his right hand to his eyes, pressing the bridge of his nose. As he pressed in, hard, he leaned back and took a deep breath, a breath harsh and dry. Then he snapped his hand away as he breathed out, and rocked the chair forward with a crash, and the office door kicked open and Doyle and Bodie tramped in. They looked worn around the edges, but they had shaved at some time, and changed into their working kit, and they looked a little happier.

'The pimp talked,' said Doyle.

'And?'

'Simon Culver. A procurer of girls and drugs and anything else you fancy. Like setting up a badger job.'

Cowley nodded and stood up. He started around the desk.

'And people in that line of business are experts at setting up blackmail schemes. We shall see what this Mr Simon Culver can tell us about this mess. He will be happy, I feel sure, to unburden his tormented little soul.'

They took Bodie's Lagonda. Nesbit's shots had damaged the tyres only, and Bodie, using his special connections with his favourite garage in Chelsea – they kept trying to sell him an Aston-Martin which, they said, was streets ahead of anything else on the road – had soon put the car back into roadworthy shape. If that idiot had hit the bodywork . . . It didn't bear contemplation. Bodie had taken some ribbing from Doyle about his car, things like: 'Why don't you paint it up and tart it about a bit? You could put it in the Chelsea Cruise.' And: 'That Saturday night is a bedlam – pity the poor coppers then. Just your style, Bodie.'

'Waste of petrol,' Cowley had said in his brusquest fashion.

'Oh, I don't know, sir,' objected Bodie. 'They had to have somewhere to show off their creations.'

'If they stop me from getting through on a case – '

'Ah, but, then, they don't know you like we do.'

Now, as they drove through the early morning London streets, Doyle's mood was sombre. Bodie could see the introspection in his partner like some mismic cloud hovering over his head. If Ray Doyle started to blame himself for what had happened, then Bodie would have to take some very sharp and salutary action, indeed . . .

Doyle started to lead up to that very situation as he said:

'That's why Ann was trying to find me.'

'You,' said Bodie firmly, 'don't know that.'

'*I* know it!' Doyle hunched forward on the back seat, what there was of it. 'A million to one chance. They need a girl, and find Ann Seaford's daughter. That's why she was trying to find me. She needed help.'

Cowley, equally thoughtful, yet with his thoughts centred on the implications, the possibilities of what might happen rather than mulling over what had happened, said: 'They needed a girl for a blackmail job. And the victim . . . ?'

He deliberately let his words trail off. Like Bodie, he wanted to shake Ray Doyle out of his dark mood.

But it was Bodie who said: 'The victim – someone with the P.M.'s private number?'

Bodie drove fast and well through steadily-filling streets. But the morning was still too young for very much traffic and the King's Road, which he negotiated with some aplomb, and a sarcastic comment to Doyle about the Chelsea Cruise, presented no problems. Culver's place was situated in an old but modernised block to the north of the Hammersmith Road, behind Olympia. The area was a maze of back alleys and short side roads. Doyle knew the area pretty well and Bodie was content to let the ex-detective constable pilot him. The Lagonda fled along the almost-aired streets – and Cowley fretted away in his head through that damnable list of people who had access to that particular private telephone number.

Sara lunged the all-black Capri half on to the pavement. The front bumper crunched into a light standard which chose that moment to blink off, its night's work over. Sara dragged the car keys from the ignition and half-fell, half-leaped from the car, leaving the driver's-side door gaping open. She ran panting into the block and up the stone stairs. At Culver's door she halted, gasping, and then started to fumble through the mess of keys hooked to the fancy key-ring. At last she found the right one and turned it, pushing the door open with her whole body, burst into the apartment.

Desperately, needing a fix so as to stop the burning that threatened to engulf her whole body and mind, she started to tear the place apart.

Bodie brought the Lagonda to a smooth stop on the other side of the street. Doyle looked through the rear window and said: 'That's the place.'

'And that,' said Bodie, nodding to the Capri, 'is the car I

saw earlier. If we'd got the confounded number we'd have been quicker – '

'Well, we didn't,' said Cowley. 'And someone arrived in a hurry.' He scanned the street. 'All right – check it out – '

Bodie and Doyle started to open their doors. They checked into instant immobility as Cowley's voice blasted at them.

'Wait!'

A large and highly-polished Jaguar with an S registration hauled in behind the Capri. Two men emerged, two large, hard-looking men in smart clothes. They moved with that stiff-legged, purposeful gait the C.I.5 men recognised as belonging to men in a certain profession, halted briefly to look in at the Capri, and then hurried into the building.

George Cowley looked at them, at the two men, studying their faces.

He checked. He felt the shock. He had not expected anything like this – a murder, a poor naked hooker in the Thames. A pimp. A blackmail job. A girl used as a pawn – but the particular private telephone number should have brought his antennae up, quivering.

He got over the shock. He fought off the stunned sensation.

'My God!' said Cowley. Then: 'Move! *Move!*'

Bodie and Doyle caught the words, the tone of voice, and they were out of the car and haring across the road. Cowley limped after them, cursing that damned leg, cursing the abrupt and diabolical implications – the vast horizons so suddenly and bleakly opened up.

Doyle and Bodie broke into the entrance way and started up the stairs. Looking up they saw the two men above them.

In the next instant the men above started shooting. Automatic fire blazed down the stairwell. Instinctively, Bodie and Doyle leaped sideways, rolling into cover of the iron banisters. The shots ploughed into the stone stairs and gouged chunks out of the walls. The very suddenness of that blast of fire would have cut down men with slower reflexes. Only a professional would have saved his life in that storm of gunfire.

Dust streaked beneath the stairs. A fresh burst of gunfire clattered in echoing thunder down the well. Chips of brick-work flew. The taste of brick dust abruptly powdered their tongues.

Cowley slid in beside them. The gunfire ceased. The distant sound of feet clattering up the stairs drifted down. Bodie and Doyle reached in for their guns.

Cowley surveyed his two agents. He nodded his head up.

'You are now dealing with pros. The big one – that is Terkoff. K.G.B.'

'Oh,' said Doyle.

'Nice to know,' said Bodie.

Then, their guns in their fists, they were up and springing for the stairs, belting up them three at a time.

The big, dark, overbearing man, the man with the suppressed violence seething within him ready to burst evilly into des-truction at the least opposition, the man Terkoff of the K.G.B., blew the lock off the door and burst in. A single fierce look, a panning glance, told him everything. A cocaine-dropper lay abandoned in the centre of the room. The win-dow was open, its curtains flapping. Terkoff sprinted across and looked out. The fire escape strung its metal spiderwork down the side of the building.

The bitch of a girl had gone down there, then. With grim purpose Terkoff climbed out the window, started down the fire escape. A last glance back showed him Baker just run-ning up to the door of the room. Then like a tiger after prey, Terkoff jumped on to the iron treads.

The two C.I.5 men reached the corridor in time to see one of the men who had been shooting at them turn to run into a doorway. The door cast a lozenge of light across the corridor floor and walls. The man stood for a moment silhouetted in that light.

'Hold it!' bellowed Doyle. 'Hold it right there!'

Baker span about, and as he turned he was already shooting. Spurts of flame lanced from the gun muzzle and the smoke blatted away.

As one, Doyle and Bodie dropped, their handguns whipping up. Two shots crashed out in a single concussion.

Baker reared up. The gun span and dropped from his nerveless fingers. He staggered back, twisting, turning, toppling into the room. His gaze raked towards the window where Terkoff's face just showed. Baker half-lifted a hand, the fingers clawing, pleading, and the other hand scrabbled at his chest where the blood oozed.

Terkoff saw Baker was done for. Without another wasted second he raced down the iron treads of the fire escape.

Bodie and Doyle leaped along the corridor. One each side of the open door – Doyle low, Bodie high – a brief instant to draw a lung-straining gulp of air, that quick-silver flash of understanding between them – the pounce with guns up, knees bent, smashing into the room ready to blast the first lethal movement from within. They thundered in and then hauled up. The room lay empty before them, the curtains blowing at the open window.

From the window they were just in time to spot Terkoff leaping off the bottom rung of the ladder, giving it no time to swing down under his weight into proper position. He landed like a great predatory cat, was up and running around the corner in an instant. Past that corner and in a narrow-angled slot between the walls, the small frantic figure of Sara ran along the pavement, running, running, scared near-witless, running for her life.

Doyle swung over the windowsill on to the escape and started down, yelling: 'Go cut 'em off!'

Bodie nodded and belted back for the door.

Half-way down the stone stairs he whistled past Cowley who was limping up and fuming in the most horrible way, grim and determined, cursing that damned bad leg.

'The girl!' yelled Bodie, springing past and careering on. 'He's after the girl!'

'Bodie!' yelped Cowley. But Bodie was already way down the stairs, crashing on. Viciously, Cowley turned around and started to hop back down the stairs.

Doyle hit the pavement with knees flexed, body bent, head up and gun snouting. Like Spring-Heel Jack he was up and sprinting instantly. The whole area was a mad tangle of back alleys and dead-end streets, with the yawning caverns slotted between high featureless walls, with dusty fly-blown windows permanently closed, with the TV aerials way up high, scraping the underside of Heaven. The sun angled down in drifting rays of light; but most of the area shrank into the deep shadows. Doyle could hear the heavy footfalls of Terkoff slapping the pavement ahead. He belted on after, checking at the corners, haring on.

Sara ran with a hip-wiggling stance that belied her turn of speed. She had lost her shoes. She ran blindly, knocking into overflowing dustbins, almost smashing into the back of one of the many parked trucks and decrepit cars. She could see no one. She was terrified. The shooting had half-paralysed her.

That man – that awful man! He had said he was going to kill her, and Uncle Sam must have agreed. It was a nightmare and all she could do was run and run and try to ignore the scarlet pains clawing at her chest, the breath rasping through her throat. She ran, and Terkoff ran swiftly after her, like a predatory hunting animal, feral, deadly, ready to kill without mercy.

Bodie hit the street and started off across the side street, running with that smooth economy of effort that came from much experience. He swung into the stance as he breasted an open alleyway. Nothing. The chase must be along there, somewhere . . . At the next alleyway he swung his gun up, ready to cut loose – nothing . . . He ran on like stink, belting for the next alley.

Sara saw the mouth of the alley ahead, with a leaning lamp post on the corner, a pile of garbage, a truck with only

8

three wheels. She turned in, gasping, rushing along blindly. A blank brick wall towered up at the end. The bricks were mouldering, crumbling, their edges black with grime. A narrow blue-painted door set in one corner . . . She reached the door, grabbed for the handle. The door did not budge. She rattled the handle frantically. Heavy footfalls sounded at her back.

With a despairing glance around, trapped, Sara flung herself about. Her breasts shook with her panting, her hair swung about her face, her lips trembled.

That awful man – he would kill her! Hide – she must hide . . .

The stinking heap of refuse – old cans, petrol tins, newspapers baled with wire, egg cartons, plastic refuse, cardboard boxes – she dropped to her knees and burrowed under the pile in the corner, hardly noticing the stink, shaking, trying to hold still, trying to stop from screaming and screaming . . .

Terkoff swung into the alley.

He was a professional. He eyed that unscalable wall. He saw the closed door. Then he saw the pile of refuse. The garbage moved, fractionally, an egg carton toppled.

Terkoff did not smile. But he lifted the Walther just that little bit higher and started to stalk down into the alley. He had the girl, Sara. He would kill her. Then no one would have a lead on him.

Abruptly he halted, standing stock still, listening.

Footfalls sounded from the street, heading up to the alley fast. Terkoff moved further in, quietly, turned, planted his feet, put both hands to the Walther, in the stance, waited, the gun aimed at the gaping mouth of the alley. No emotion whatsoever crossed that dark, implacable face. The gun muzzle held unerringly on the alley mouth.

Ray Doyle whipped around the next corner fast into the alley and saw the whole set-up. No time to curse, no time to berate himself for the biggest sucker in the business. He saw the dark squared-off form, the stance, saw the Walther

114

lifted. Just time to fling himself sideways.

Just time to – Terkoff's gun fired.

The bullet slammed into Doyle's thigh, spinning him away.

His time had run out. He was still in the air, half-launching himself and half-struck by the momentum of the bullet. Doyle snapped off a quick one, a shot compounded of all the innate marksmanship in him, the swift sizing up of the situation, the guts of shooting when the thumping impact of the slug battered that first wave-shock of pain through him.

His S&W .357 Magnum blatted. The slug took Terkoff in the chest.

Stunned, shocked, Terkoff staggered.

He had hit the bastard, shot him, and the man had shot back in the instant he fell.

Terkoff took a breath, a deep, deep breath, holding on to his swimming senses. He saw the man had fallen. Saw the gun had spilled from his hand, toppled a few feet away from him. Terkoff turned. There was a job he had to finish. He started to walk towards the heap of garbage, and each step was like wading through molasses, hard, tacky, a tremendous effort of will.

Doyle lay on the sleazy ground. Dirty water puddled near his head. He stretched out his hand. He was going to pass out any second. He tried to reach the gun. He could not make it. He tried. He tried to force himself to move his body, his hand and arm outstretched, the fingers straining towards the S&W. But he knew he would never make it.

With all those dark secret reserves of will summoned in this climactic moment, Terkoff made himself walk down the alley towards the heap of stinking garbage. He had one shot. He reached the garbage. With a last, awful demonstration of will-power he kicked. A collapsed cardboard box slid away, egg cartons toppled. The white, frightened face of Sara showed, staring up at him, with those big blue eyes wide in horror.

Slowly, deliberately, determined to use the last shot and

115

finish the thing, Terkoff raised his gun.

Ray Doyle saw. The world lay on its side, distorted, contracting and expanding. But he saw. His groping fingers closed inches short of the S&W. He forced himself, and his body did not obey his mind. He lay there, on the stinking ground, and saw Terkoff's gun lift to bear down on Ann Seaford's daughter.

Two feet in elegant English leather shoes, highly polished, appeared in Doyle's despairing vision. A pair of legs impeccably clad in the best English tailoring seemed to his distorted vision to tower up and up. He heard a gun fire a single shot, and he knew it was a Browning 9 mm Hi-Power.

Terkoff stood up. He arched his back. His arms jerked out, and the Walther automatic revolved weirdly on his finger, slid, toppled to the ground. Terkoff stood, transfixed, unmoving. He shuddered, suddenly, shaking, turning, folding, collapsing. He fell. His face smashed into the filthy muck of the garbage pile. His head crunched into the garbage. His wide-open, staring eyes glared awfully into the petrified blue eyes of Ann Seaford's daughter.

For two heartbeats nothing moved.

Then Bodie, the Browning still at the ready, looked down on Doyle.

'Ray –'

'The girl!' Doyle husked the words. 'Get the girl!'

Bodie nodded and started up the alley. The Lagonda screeched across the mouth of the alley and slewed to a tyre-crunching stop. Cowley hopped out, fuming, gun already in his fist. He took a single look at Doyle and then went limping, licketty-split, up the alley after Bodie.

Bodie gently lifted Sara. She clung to him, her hair hanging, her face working, sobbing. Bodie held her close for a moment, turning her face away from the corpse in the garbage. The shock was working on her now, her paralysis leaving her. Bodie held her, turning her, anxious to get her away and anxious to get back to the mouth of the alley.

He saw Cowley turning the dead body of Terkoff over.

Cowley looked up as Bodie went past.

'Terkoff,' said Cowley. 'He was a good man.'

'Yeah!' flared Bodie. 'Well – there's a *better* man back there!'

When they got back to Doyle he had managed to sit up and strap his leather belt around his thigh. He was pulling it tight as they stopped by him. The tourniquet would hold until they got him to dock. He looked up. He did not feel like smiling.

'You all right, Doyle?' Cowley made it sharp, hard, matter of fact.

Doyle nodded. It was time to show them he wasn't dead yet – although he damned well nearly had been.

'Well,' said Ray Doyle. 'I won't have your trouble. The slug came out the other side.'

Ray Doyle insisted on going to the funeral. Bodie was fully prepared to start a highly-unpleasant session convincing Doyle that he was not to blame for Ann Seaford's death. But the ex-detective did not raise the subject openly. Bodie, for all the badinage and ribbing that went between them, had too high a regard – and respect – for his partner to open it up himself. Doyle was grown-up now. He could handle it.

The gravestone was simple, tasteful, set among many others in their serried plots. The breeze blew the first scattering of orange-gold leaves across the graves. The flowers looked bright and colourful, and yet could only give a pathetic and inadequate feeling. Doyle leaned on his stick and looked down on the grave.

The headstone read:

IN MEMORY OF ANN SEAFORD

Finally, using his stick because he had to, Doyle turned away. He started to walk along the gravel between the white monuments. Tall cypresses moved in the breeze. Bodie shoved upright from the tombstone on which he had been leaning and fell into step beside his partner – a tricky operation as Doyle limped along. Bodie decided this was the time, enough was enough.

'Be a big plus with the girls, Doyle.' He stabbed a finger at the stick. 'That stick of yours. I know you'll get rid of it just as soon as you can, before you should. But – you can fabricate a bit.'

Doyle regarded him impassively; but they both knew they were warming up again, getting back to Bodie and Doyle, pushing events away behind them.

'Sure,' said Bodie. 'You can invent some story. Say you got it ski-jumping or whatever. You can pretend you got it doing something really dangerous.'

Chapter Ten

Sir Arden French was dying.

He lay laxly in his wide bed, a man who had once been a power, blessed with a golden tongue and a commanding presence, a memory that devastated those less-well briefed. Now he was shrunken, wasted away. And, yet, he was only seventy-five. In his tastefully luxurious house in a select Georgian square in the best part of London, surrounded by old friends, Sir Arden was on the point of appearing before the last and greatest tribunal of all.

Now Sir Arden weakly gripped the hand of the priest who bent over the bed.

In the room were a number of Sir Arden's associates, calm, dignified men, and Lord Derrington, a magnificent lion-headed man who, although sixty-odd looked fifteen years younger. With him Sir Charles Milvern stood quietly, watching the bed, apparently composed despite the seething currents of fear and horror that possessed him, driving him almost mad with worry – and yet, at the same time, driving him on to the course he knew he would have to take.

Eddy Turner, who had retired as a detective superintendent with the active and monetary help of Sir Arden, looked down impassively. The man had been a friend, a good friend, and Turner's career and life of comparative luxury after he'd retired were owed to him.

Now the priest moved nearer, speaking softly.

'Sir Arden . . . Sir Arden – is there anything else you wish to tell me?'

The dying man's head moved from side to side, weakly. He struggled to speak, two spots of colour in his cheeks turning his face corpse-white. A little puff of air burst from his crimped lips. He moaned, a low, burr of sound, and then said in a hushed, choked voice: 'Suzy. Suzy Carter . . . '

Eddy Turner clammed his jaws together. He stared fixedly at the dying man.

Sir Arden French gripped the priest's hand now with the frenetic energy of approaching death. He half-pulled himself up. His face looked glazed, wild, desperate. 'Suzy Carter . . . I killed her. I killed Suzy Carter.'

The men in the room looked down, not quite sure what to do or say, embarrassed. Lord Derrington frowned, casting a quick glance at Turner as the ex-detective superintendent made a sudden, involuntary step forward.

'I killed – ' Sir Arden gulped, clawing now at the priest. 'I killed Suzy Car – '

He could say no more. He slumped back. He shuddered, a long fluttering sigh, his eyelids closed, and his whole body relaxed in death.

In that moment of release everyone remained stock still. Sir Charles Milvern looked at Lord Derrington, waiting for a lead. Eddy Turner moved. He walked stiffly to the door, his head up, his shoulders back, went out quickly, without saying a word.

When Sir Charles Milvern returned to his plush Victoria suite of offices Jessica told him that Mr Cowley wished to see him. At his desk, very much the coming man of affairs, Milvern looked up as Jessica ushered Cowley in. Cowley limped across the thick carpet to the desk.

'Ah, Cowley,' said Milvern. 'Long time no see. What can I do for you?'

The chief of C.I.5 placed a document on the desk and stood looking ruminatively at Milvern.

'An urgent document that requires your signature, Sir Charles.'

'Of course.' Milvern picked up his pen, unscrewed the cap, poised, ready to sign, scanning the document quickly. Before he had read a half dozen lines he looked up. His face flushed painfully. 'Is this some kind of joke?'

Cowley shook his head. The motion was slow, deliberately meaningful. 'I drafted the document myself. I thought it perfectly clear. "Ill health is forcing you to announce your retirement from public life . . ." '

'My ill health? What the devil – ?'

'The Devil? Yes. Yes, I think he had something to do with it.'

As he spoke Cowley shook out a handful of photographs from an envelope and placed them face-up on the desk. The babyish face, and then the infant's face, and then the almost-mature face of Sara, Ann Seaford's daughter, stared up at Milvern. The blood drained from his cheeks. Milvern just sat, a stricken lump, glaring at the damning photos.

Cowley retrieved the pictures and said: 'You'll notice the document has been endorsed by both the Prime Minister and your own party leader.'

The expensive fountain pen fell from Milvern's limp fingers. Cowley picked it up and extended it.

'Enjoy your retirement, Sir Charles.'

Broken, Sir Charles Milvern took the pen.

Eddy Turner couldn't sleep. He'd returned home straight away to his nice house on the outskirts of Harrogate, where he almost belonged. The house set him apart from most of his old friends. The money had done a lot for him and Ellie. Eddy and Ellie Turner. They'd had a good life – ever since the Coronation. Funny, that was the way he'd always remember it, the Coronation and Everest, Sherpa Tensing and Hillary.

He was sleeping, yet he wasn't sleeping. Ellie lay at his side in her nice new nightgown, breathing long and slow. But Eddy Turner's closed eyelids brought back to him again and again that night twenty-five years ago. He could feel again the paper in his hands, and the headlines, the smell of the small anonymous hotel.

Hamer had been standing guard that night.

Turner's closed eyelids could not stop the scenes of twenty-five years ago from unreeling, all over again, a never-ending film that flickered luridly, flickered with the pulses of the memories in his own brain.

He'd walked along that hotel corridor, smelling the dust and the indefinable hotel smells, walked on knowing exactly what he was going to do – what he *had* to do.

Hamer was reading the paper. He lowered it smartly enough when his superior officer said:

'Everything okay, Hamer?'

He didn't much care for Hamer. The man sat there on his tilted-back chair, his jacket off revealing the shoulder holster with its new, yellowish straps. Guns and the cops didn't mix as easily then as now.

'She's still in one piece, sir.' Then Hamer indicated the paper. 'Nice about Everest. Just in time for the Coronation.'

The paper's title logo had been printed in gold. A big picture of the Queen's coronation gown dominated the front page, with the screamer: THE QUEEN'S SURPRISE! THIS IS THE GOLDEN DAY. The weather had been foul, and the paper had predicted: EVERYTHING BUT SNOW. Over on the right column the beginning of a story was headlined EVEREST IS CONQUERED.

'The British expedition has conquered "unconquerable" Everest, the world's highest mountain.'

Turner's own paper carried the story, too – he slapped it against his thigh. 'Yes. Very nice. Bloody cold for 'em, up there – nearly as bad as this. You check the emergency exits?'

'Not recently.' Hamer folded the paper, revealing a large picture of crowds building up under the lions in Trafalgar Square, under the headline: AT THE LION'S FEET. The front page story continued under the headline: EVEREST BEATEN AT LAST. Hamer stood up, tucking the paper under his arm by the new yellow revolver holster. 'Think it's about time I should?'

Turner nodded sourly. 'Exactly about time.'

'Yes, sir,' said Hamer, and went off down the corridor to carry out his routine check. Turner watched him until he was out of sight and then pushed open the bedroom door. He went in quietly.

Two women stood in the hotel bedroom. Policewoman Ann Berry rose as Turner entered, and her hand dropped away from the shoulder holster she wore. She had removed her uniform jacket. She was attractive, about thirty or so, Junoesque, full-fleshed, highly sexed – or so Turner guessed. She presented a contrast to the girl who stood looking out of the window.

This girl's slight, slender form with the fair silky hair, her stance by the big window, the droop to her shoulders – none of these things must matter. Turner looked at Ann Berry. His eyes were hard. Ann stared back for a moment, then, with a slight – the very slightest – lift of her shoulders, turned away.

Turner could not see the girl's face. That was a blessing.

He crossed the room soundlessly. The big window was open, the sounds of revelry blowing up from the streets far below. They would all get as drunk as lords out there tonight, sloshed out of their skulls. Coronations didn't happen all that often, and what with Everest, too – and there was always bloody Korea – well, letting the hair down came as a relief.

Turner stood behind the fair-haired girl. She started to turn, hearing his breathing he could not control. He grabbed her shoulders. He pushed her forward. A shocked and animal-like scream burst from her throat. Turner pushed – hard – opening his hands. She toppled for an instant in the window, half-turned, screaming, her arms flailing, her fair silky hair swirling.

Then she fell.

Suzy Carter fell from the window and splattered on the pavement beneath.

Turner's half-dream, half-nightmare exploded.

He rocketed up in the comfortable bed, shouting, sweating, shaking.

'*Suzy – !*'

Ellie Turner sat up as though shot. She reached across an arm from the nice new nightgown and snapped the bedside lamp on. The roseate glow spread upon the sweating, shocked face of her husband, glaring emptily into the bedroom.

'Eddy . . . ? Eddy!'

She gripped his arm and shook him. She felt frightened, and the fear was worse because she knew that there was something here to fear and she did not know what it was.

'What's wrong? Eddy!'

'Nothing. Nothing.'

Turner's voice slurred. He spoke, waking up, still half-drugged, still shattered by that ghastly vision of the past.

Ellie Turner looked at him, hard. Her mouth firmed.

'That nightmare again –'

'I told you. I'm all right!'

'You haven't had that dream for years.' Ellie looked at him now, studying him, seeing the way the fat had built up, looking at him almost as a stranger. 'Not for years. You seemed to have got over whatever it was. But it was different this time. You were shouting out a name. *Her* name. Suzy Carter.'

As Bodie had direfully predicted, Ray Doyle got rid of his walking stick before it was seemly, and he went hopping and limping along the corridor in the anonymous building off Whitehall housing C.I.5. He had made a sharpish recovery, though, for which Bodie was as pleased as he was. But they were off ops for a space. The sound of quick footsteps behind them made them both half-turn – that was sheer simple survival – and then swing back, smiling.

Tony Bastable, still as eager, still as handsome, charged up and clapped a friendly hand on each shoulder, right and left.

'Hey, fellers! I made it! Cowley gave me my first assignment.'

Doyle said in a neutral voice: 'Cowley?'

Bodie, acting very seriously, said: 'I think he means *Mister* Cowley. D'you think we should report him for insubordination?'

Doyle, equally seriously, said, musingly: 'Should do.'

'He'll pull him off the assignment, of course.'

'Of course.' The gravity of these two nearly choked them up. 'Might even kick him out altogether.'

Tony betrayed extreme alarm at this. 'You're kidding!' He saw their grave faces, and although he'd been warned about these two, about Bodie and Doyle, he felt the premonitory kick of real alarm hit him under the ribs. 'You *are* kidding?'

'You have, Tony,' said Bodie, 'to be with C.I.5 a helluva long time before you get to call Mister Cowley just Cowley. And then it ain't wise so to do. Not wise at all.'

'And,' said Doyle, smiling at last, 'even then not actually in the building. He's got ears like a hawk.'

'Eyes,' said Bodie. And as Doyle flicked him an eyebrow raiser, said primly: 'Hawks have eyes.'

'They have ears too, don't they? And good ones. Did you ever see a hawk wearing a deaf aid?'

Tony stared at them uncertain, realising he was still the new boy, and yet eagerly determined to be in with the crew.

'Don't you want to know about my assignment?'

'Stake out up north,' said Bodie, casually. 'We read about it on the duty board.' He started to move off with his partner, arguing as always. '*Eyes* like a hawk is a simile. Now for *ears*, you'd have to choose – '

'An elephant?'

'Why an elephant?' Bodie half-turned in the middle of the wrangle, to say: 'Oh, have fun, Tony.'

Doyle nodded. 'And good luck.' He went back to the serious business of getting under his partner's skin. 'Well, elephants have *big* ears.'

Tony watched them as they went off, and Bodie said: 'And

good eyes, too. Well, have you ever seen an elephant wearing glasses?'

When Betty showed Lord Derrington into the drab C.I.5 office, Cowley prepared himself. He held a lively respect and admiration for this lion-headed man, nurtured over some years of mutual co-operation out in the West Indies. 'Lord Derrington –'

'George!' said Derrington, walking forward to shake hands. 'And, please, let's drop the "lord" bit. You've no idea how much it embarrasses me.'

'Not judging from the social columns I haven't. It seems to sit well on you – er – Peter.'

'Peter – yes, that's better. You look a bit grey, George. The leg?'

'Is still attached to my body.' Nobody got special treatment from Cowley where that damned leg of his was concerned.

The two men sat down and Derrington said: 'It must be, what, seven years? Georgetown, wasn't it?'

'Eight,' said Cowley. 'Thomasville.' At Derrington's swiftly concealed abashed expression, Cowley said quickly: 'But how could you be expected to remember. It was a long time ago.'

'You remembered.'

'I've reason. You taught me a great deal, Peter, about protocol and bureaucracy, things I'm inclined to ride rough-shod –'

'Yes, that was always your forte, George, cutting corners. That's why I'm here. You heard about Sir Arden French?'

'Yes. I understand it was a happy release.'

'For him? Or the men under him?' He looked closely at Cowley, and went on: 'My irreverence shocks you?'

'Nothing shocks me. And I know Sir Arden ruled Internal Security with a rod of iron.'

Leaning forward, Derrington said: 'I killed Suzy Carter.' He held up a hand, and Cowley listened. 'Those were Sir Arden's dying words. You didn't know? Well, they *would* cover it up, wouldn't they? A security chief's final admission

126

– But I don't want it covered up, George. I want to know.'

'Know what?'

'What he meant. If a Suzy Carter actually existed. What's behind it. I want you – C.I.5 – to find out.'

'But, surely – His own department?'

'Might have many reasons not to investigate further.'

'Special Branch – '

'Work hand in glove with Sir Adrian's department. I've discussed it with the P.M. and he – *we* – feel that you – and only you – are equipped to ferret this one out.'

Reflectively, Cowley said: 'Suzy Carter . . .'

Doyle and Bodie caught the job of sorting through the files. They made suitable nasty remarks; but they did the job and reported back to Cowley. He listened, and then said: 'What do you mean, missing?'

'Well,' said Bodie, feeling hurt. 'Sort of like – *gone*. Disappeared. Taken.'

Doyle confirmed his partner's acid comments. 'The file sections at records had the Carter S. files all neatly organised – save this one. It was in 1953. Suzy Carter was a prosecution witness for some kind of corruption bust. We've ordered up the daily papers for the time, should give us more details.'

'What happened to Suzy Carter?' demanded Cowley.

'She thought she was Icarus,' said Bodie.

Doyle got in quickly: 'Jumped out of a window. Before she could testify.'

'Jumped?'

The partners looked at their chief. All three felt their noses twitching. 'That's the official story,' said Bodie.

'The officer in charge of the case – ?'

'Was Detective Superintendent Turner,' cut in Doyle. 'Retired nine years ago. We have an address; but it's up north.'

'Who do we have up north just now?'

As one, Bodie and Doyle said: 'Tony Bastable.'

Curtly, with a commanding nod, Cowley said: 'Call him. Tell him to bring Turner in.' As the partners turned to go out, Cowley picked up the phone. 'Peter was right,' he said, and then, into the phone: 'Get me Lord Derrington.'

It was late when Tony Bastable pulled up in his brand new Vauxhall and stepped out. The house on the outskirts of Harrogate had been difficult to find; but here it was, and Tony walked up the drive and rang the bell. He stepped back from the door a way and opened his coat. The Colt Python was securely holstered. Young, brash, confident and eager, the brand new C.I.5 agent waited as lights went on deep in the house and slow steps shuffled to the door.

The door opened and Turner stood there, just tying the cord around his dressing gown, his hair – what there was of it – tousled, blinking sleepily. He hadn't slept well for that frightening nightmare.

'Yes?'

'Ex-Detective Superintendent Turner?'

'Yes – yes – '

Tony took out his I.D. and showed it in the hall light. Turner blinked. 'C.I.5?'

'Mister Cowley would like to have a word with – '

Tony's polite words were blotted out in the shattering bellow of a shotgun. Turner was picked up and hurled back by the blast, the bunched shot scything through him, blowing him away, showering the opening door with blood. Instantly, Tony swung away from the door, his hand diving to come up with the Python. He was good. He caught a vague glimpse of a shadowed shape by the rose bushes and his left hand swept in to grip his right and lift the handgun. He had a weird fragmentary memory of Ray Doyle and Bodie, joshing him about going into the stance with a two-handed grip to shoot, and time, when the second shotgun muzzle blew its load of death into his guts.

Tony Bastable went backwards, showering blood, smashed across Turner's threshold and across the bloody corpse of the man he had come to see, the man whose death had caused his own.

Somewhere in the night a dog began to bark.

Presently a car engine started up and soon faded.

An upstairs window opened and Ellie Turner's voice floated down, echoing in the night.

'Eddy? Eddy?'

Chapter Eleven

Tony Bastable's body was brought back through London en route for Portsmouth, for Tony had been of naval folk. Cowley, Bodie and Doyle went to see their fellow agent off, standing silent and grim in the chill stone place, with the coffined body between them, Dick Mason and Tully Crabtree, Jim Bain and Bill Wesley, the others, those not on duty, attended this stupid, silly, really unnecessary parting ceremony. There would be no attendance at the funeral for them. They had other things to do – things that Tony would have approved of.

Cowley stood a little apart from his men.

He stood square and blocky, a little hunched, his head thrust down, his fists driven deeply into the pocket of his light topcoat. His face with its lines and creases, its sandy hair, looked drawn, tired and exhausted, and yet vicious.

Abruptly, he looked up.

These men of his, the Action Squad, the Big A – they were saying goodbye to a fellow operative. He was saying goodbye to a young man whom he had selected, hand-picked, trained up – the fault, of course, was Cowley's. Tony hadn't been ready. And yet – and yet the indications at the scene of the crime told the pitiful story. There had been no chance, no *time* ...

Cowley stared deeply at his men.

'Suzy Carter,' he said. His voice sounded like ice floes grating together in congealed water. 'I want her from cradle to grave!'

Mason and Crabtree reported in from Harrogate and Betty took down their statement over the phone in her impeccable one hundred and twenty plus words a minute shorthand. She rang off and went into Cowley's office, taking with her the old newspapers that had just come through.

Turner, an ex-detective superintendent, owned a Rolls-Royce. He had speculated. The money, Mrs Turner said, came to them in a windfall in 1953. He had been troubled by nightmares at one time; they had ceased but had latterly returned. He called the name Suzy Carter in his sleep.

Cowley said, with a chill evil in his manner: 'Eddy Turner had nearly sixty-five years of life. With a Rolls in the garage. Tony Bastable was just twenty-six.'

Bodie and Doyle sat in the uncomfortable office chairs as Betty handed around the old newspapers. 'Star Hotel, Bayswater,' she said. 'The night of Tuesday, the second of June, 1953 . . . Out of a ninth floor window. It only made a by-line. Too much else going on that day.'

'I'll tell you something,' said Bodie. 'Did you know Coronation red is the secret of whiter teeth?'

'A report of the stabbing of a teenage girl – Barbara Songhurst, stabbed four times, found in the Thames near Twickenham. And Christine Reed still missing – ' Doyle nodded. 'We know that one.'

'I see Jane's kept all her clothes on.' Bodie riffled through the pages.

Cowley looked across at Doyle.

'Are you all through imitating me, Doyle?'

'Yes, sir.'

'Then you and Bodie get on this. I want it taken apart.'

The partners rose to go. As they went out, Doyle said: '. . . and Everest was also conquered.'

The Star Hotel. The room. This was the room where Suzy Carter had fallen to her death. The hotel was due for demolition. Wallpaper hung peeling, dust puffed as they moved, the ceiling light was worn away from its rose. The big window opened with a squeaking groan as Bodie shoved. The two looked out and down.

Bodie said, consulting the papers he carried: 'Police had moved her here for her own protection. She was due to testify the next day.'

Doyle looked around. 'Testify to what?'

'Corruption . . . Neil Turvey Combines. A finger in many pies. Government building contracts. Talk of bribes to the tune of ten million. A Watergate in the making . . .'

'Ten million?' said Doyle. 'That's a lot of loot.'

'Yeah – and a helluva lot more then. Suzy Carter worked for Turvey Combines.'

'So she knew where the body was buried.'

Bodie leaned on the window sill. He looked out. 'Ten million. Would you push a girl out of a window for ten million?'

Doyle stared down. His face showed no expression. 'Is that a definite offer?'

The drop down the nine floors looked a long cold way. Bodie squinted down at the ground beneath. 'She didn't make much of a splash in the papers,' he said. 'But I'll bet –'

Doyle swung in and stared hard at his partner. He shook his head. 'You know, Bodie, before I met you I thought "black humour" meant the Kentucky Minstrels.'

The old hotel due for demolition, the room – the fatal room where Suzy Carter had spent her last hours, the long drop to the unyielding ground, these had given the partners a feel for the case. They could imagine her tenseness, her fear, the armed policemen, the shivery sensation of killers out to silence her testimony. Yes, she had been a fragile, lonely, frightened girl. And some bastard had pushed her out of the window. And some other bastard had had her pushed.

They reported back to Cowley. He had the papers spread out, going over them again. Whoever had removed the files on Carter S. Whoever had ordered the girl murdered, must still be active. Cowley looked up as the partners came in, and he got right to the point.

'Sir Arden French wasn't Sir Arden then. Just plain Arden French, defence attorney for the Turvey Combines.'

'And now he's dead,' said Bodie. 'Claiming he killed Suzy.'

'And Turner's dead,' said Cowley.

A little, charged, silence followed. Then, gently, drifting with the conversation, Doyle pointed out: 'Neil Turvey's still alive.'

'No,' said Cowley. 'You lay off Turvey. He came out of that affair lily white and roses . . .'

'Because,' pursued Doyle. 'The main witness was conveniently pushed out of a window.'

'We don't know she was pushed – yet. Until we do, remember, Turvey's more important, more influential now than he ever was. You lay off him, understand? For the time being, anyway.' Cowley slapped the papers before him. 'Ann Berry. The police woman who was supposed to be helping look after Suzy Carter.'

Bodie and Doyle rose and walked out. Bodie saw how Doyle was forcing himself not to limp. Cowley saw, too. So did Betty. Nobody gave Cowley competition – not even in limping.

ANN BERRY'S HOLIDAY HOME FOR DOGS read the sign as Bodie brought his gleaming Lagonda through the first white-painted gate. A grey-stone house with blue-slate roofs lifted into view beyond a line of trees. Hedges all neatly trimmed contained the scene. The day had remained fine and the drive down from London had passed pleasantly enough, filled with the usual banter, undershot with the tensions of the case, the knowledge that a young and defenceless girl had been callously murdered for greed – probably. Cowley was right; they didn't have enough to go on yet. But this ex-policewoman Ann Berry had been placed right at the scene of the crime. She would know. Bodie and Doyle would find out. That was a promise.

Bodie tooled the Lagonda around the curve into the driveway. The house opened up with a line of outbuildings flanking it. Parked on the gravel outside the door a beat-up Jaguar attracted their attention and then, as a man ran across to the parked car and jumped in at the driver's side, Bodie hit the accelerator. The Lagonda leaped forward. The man was wearing a dark-blue anorak and he had the hood pulled up over his head. He carried a shotgun.

A man carrying a shotgun was no great mystery in the country – but this shotgun was of the semi sawn-off variety.

The Lagonda hurtled up the drive into the turning circle. The Jaguar did not move. At the last moment the shotgun belched from over the opened offside door.

Bodie's windscreen shattered. Bits and pieces flew. Blinded he clawed at the wheel, hoping to send the car clear. The Jaguar leaped away, almost rammed the Lagonda, and then span its tyres on the gravel, shooting out stones in a fan, and sped off down the drive.

The Lagonda went into a swathing skid with Bodie fighting the wheel. Doyle ripped out his handgun and used the butt to smash away the smashed screen before them. When Bodie could see again he aligned the car with the drive and stamped on the throttle as though it was a rattler or a cottonmouth.

The Lagonda screeched down the drive for the white gate and the road.

Doyle had time to shout: 'That shotgun – Tony!'

'Yeah,' said Bodie and wrenched the wheel to hurl the car protesting on to the road.

They fouled up.

The Jaguar was waiting just past the white painted gate and the neatly-trimmed hedge. The shotgun snouted. It blasted. The Lagonda's front tyre blew and shredded away and instantly Bodie was fighting the wheel, see-sawing, trying to keep the crazy car from running amuck. The Jaguar revved up and sped away. The Lagonda hurtled on, slewing, mounted the grassy roadside bank and thumped to a chilling stop.

Bodie sat back, looking absolutely disgusted.

134

'D'you get the number?'

'No.'

'A hell of a mess! One helluva mess!'

Bodie got out of the car and surveyed the damage.

'That windscreen – that'll cost! And another tyre! I tell you, Doyle, I'm putting into the squad for a bullet-proof Lotus! Next time we use your car.'

'The house,' said Doyle. 'Hark at those dogs.'

They sprinted back across the road and up the drive between the neat-white-painted fences. The dogs' barking grew and grew, an insane ululation of primeval sound. They hared around the corner where the sound was loudest – and stopped.

On the gravel a young girl bent over another girl – a woman, this woman who lay sprawled, dead, blown away, wasted, bloody. The girl sobbed, touching the dead woman's face. She turned to stare blindly at Bodie and Doyle, her face wet with tears. She brushed at her face and created a ghastly effect as the dead woman's blood mingled with the tears and painted her face in gory colour.

'She's dead! Ann's dead!'

Ann Berry's Holiday Home for Dogs had temporarily closed its white-painted door for business. The girl – Sally – could only mumble and mutter incoherently even when the police summoned by the partners took over. A policewoman tried to soothe Sally. Bodie came back to the main hall and showed his ID and the stack of papers he had found to the Inspector.

'We're taking these, C.I.5.'

The partners left the police to what would be a most unrewarding task.

Bodie insisted on nursing his beloved Lagonda back, and the draught through the non-existent windshield ruffled the papers as Doyle studied them. 'She did not,' Bodie observed, 'have a Rolls-Royce.'

'No,' said Doyle, shuffling the papers. 'But that house set

her back a cool fifty thousand, and that was in 1955 and she paid cash.' He looked up. 'I thought you couldn't buy a house with ordinary common cash?'

'If there's enough you can buy anything. Did you notice the bedroom?'

'Yeah. Only one bed being slept in. Way back in the unpermissive fifties, a policewoman with those kinds of tendencies – '

'She'd be open to all kinds of blackmail and bribery.'

After a time Doyle hauled out a certificate and held it up.

'Jackpot!' Bodie flung him a quick look and then went back to driving. 'Share-holdings. Twenty thousand shares in Turvey Combines. Purchased in June, 1953.'

Bodie said: 'Turvey.'

They stopped off to grab a bite to eat on the way to Turvey's house. They saw the welcoming lights of a Little Chef, and as Doyle said when Bodie started to argue: 'They're okay, Bodie! We don't have to eat at the greasy spoon all our lives, coppers or not – '

'I was never a copper, Constable – '

'But I was! And detectives get used to the sausage and chips routine. The Little Chef's are okay – '

When they came out and drove on, Bodie licked his lips and said: 'For a member of the alleged smart Chelsea Set, for two members, come to that, we did all right. I feel a new man.'

Doyle favoured him with one of his cutting-to-the-quick looks, and they motored on. Bodie continued to moan about his Lagonda. 'If these bloody villains keep on shooting up Bessie – '

'Bessie?' said Doyle. 'I thought it was Lancelot?'

'I have to keep having new tyres, don't I?'

'So?'

'So I shall get mad. Real mad.'

Turvey's place turned out to be a palace. A great sprawling mansion set in extensive grounds, with a long curving drive, oozing with the signs of wealth. They showed their

IDs to the man who opened the door, and waited in the room into which they were ushered. Bodie said: 'A butler, yet.'

'Money,' said Doyle.

The sounds of rock music sounded through the door. Bodie opened the figured panelled door and looked out. In a room across the hall he saw two youngsters, all tight jeans and T-shirts, a boy and girl, fiddling with a mobile disco, a chunk of hi-fi equipment that must have set Turvey back more than half a grand. Then Turvey walked in, smiling, poised, smooth, every inch the suavely successful business tycoon.

The partners took him in. They noted him. They marked him down. Neil Turvey was around sixty-five, a still powerful man in the – as Bodie mentally phrased it – the John Wayne style. He was big with muscle only just beginning to run to fat. His hair, his manicure, his clothes, were all immaculate. His voice was superbly modulated, betraying no trace of its origins whatsoever. He walked in with a practised, vote-winning smile on his face.

'Gentlemen – '

He stopped short. Bodie and Doyle whose sartorial outfits had seen some wear of late were sprawled in chairs in relaxed, almost arrogant positions. Doyle's field-green cut-down combat jacket, and faded jeans, Bodie's expensive trousers topped by a supple leather windcheater, were not, according to the expression that altered the welcoming smile of Turvey's face, exactly out of the *Tailor and Cutter*.

Turvey gathered himself. 'My butler said – police?'

Doyle, who hugged these moments to his ex-blue-uniformed breast, proffered his ID. 'Not exactly. Doyle. He's Bodie.'

Turvey looked at the ID. 'C.I.5? A *sort* of police, then?'

Bodie made it mean something as he said: 'Not even near. Police – some of them – can be corrupted.'

The smile that had grown back on Turvey's face remained. The partners wouldn't easily faze him with tactics like that – this boyo had been around a long time. He moved to the lavishly stocked drinks bar, saying: 'You're not here to argue semantics? And I hope you don't regard a drink as the first seeds of corruption? I ask because I have a particularly good Malt Scotch here and – ' He picked up the decanter and turned, seeing their stony faces and talking imperturbably on. ' – too early? Then you won't mind if *I* – ? Good. Now, I want to help all I can.'

Doyle said: 'Help?'

Turvey spoke as though dealing with a child, or a bumbling six-week new constable in a uniform that did not fit. 'It has always been my practice to assist in the cause of law and order. If you own as much property as I do, it makes sense. My relationship with the police, and I know,' he went on, cutting over Doyle's quick reaction of protest, 'I know you're not exactly in that category. But my dealings with the police have always been very amicable.'

'I'll bet!' said Bodie – and then wished he hadn't as Turvey turned, beautifully poised, his eyebrows only barely lifting. 'I beg your pardon?'

Doyle came to his partner's assistance, and decided to lean a little. He said, putting a crisp note into his voice: 'Ann Berry.'

The tensions that simmered below the surface of this so-far one-sided exchange, if, as Doyle remarked, tensions can ever simmer – increased. Turvey knew nothing of Ann Berry. Not even an Ann Berry who had been wasted by a twelve bore. He wanted to know, politely, if the C.I.5 men were crazy – did they know how many shareholders there were in his many companies?

'Yes,' said Doyle, 'but she acquired her shares on Wednesday, the third of June, 1953. Day after the Coronation. Day after they climbed to the top of Everest.'

'Day,' snapped Bodie, 'after Suzy Carter died.'

'Suzy Carter? Who the hell's Suzy Carter?'

It was time, the mutual look of recognition between Bodie and Doyle said, it was time for the double act.

They appeared to forget the presence of the impeccably-

138

clad and distinguished-looking Turvey as they spoke.

Doyle spoke first.

'He's forgotten.

'Amnesia.

'*Convenient* amnesia.'

'It's sometimes brought on by a blow on the head.'

Doyle finished the repartee: 'And miraculously restored the same way.'

Together, the partners moved in on Turvey. They drew very close to him. It was quite clear by their faces – it was perfectly clear to Turvey – that the acting was over.

A plummy voice broke across the tension between the men in the room. 'Neil?'

Bodie and Doyle swung about. A well-dressed man, well-groomed, high of colour on port and brandy nurtured veins, stood in the doorway. He was another of these leaders of men. The partners recognised him at once, for he had headed up the Home Office Investigatory Committee – this was Sir Frederick Talon.

'Was just leaving,' said Talon, looking curiously at Bodie and Doyle. 'I'll see you at the club tonight. Everything all right?'

Turvey flashed that smile. 'Ah, Freddy – let me introduce what was it – Doyle and Bodie? C.I.5.'

'I think we've met.' Talon looked at them and then to Turvey and back. 'You work for Cowley? Give him my regards.'

Sir Frederick Talon, the amenities over, began to withdraw.

Turvey stopped him with a quietly vicious: 'Everything is not all right!' Talon stopped. Turvey went on cuttingly: 'You asked me: "Was everything all right?" It is not. These two – men – have been using Schutz-Staffeln tactics against me. *Against me,* Freddy!'

This Sir Frederick Talon was no fool – he had made quite an impact on the Committee. He looked closely at the partners.

139

'For what reason?'

'No reason,' snapped Turvey.

Bodie said: 'Suzy Carter –'

And, simultaneously, Doyle said: 'And Ann Berry – both dead . . .'

Talon spoke severely, 'And what is the connection with Mr Turvey here?'

Doyle said: 'Well – there might be. We thought –'

Bodie burst out savagely: 'We *know* –'

They were getting nowhere. Talon cut in icily.

'Is this a matter of evidence? Solid evidence? Well – *is it*?'

Bodie and Doyle looked at him. They knew they had nothing that would stand up in court. And this Sir Frederick Talon was a stickler for the rules. He saw all that in them, and his veinous face tightened up. His eyelids lowered just that fraction that portended storm warnings.

'Doyle. And Bodie. I shall remember those names.' His face looked real mean, now, and the partners knew they had blown it. Talon turned to his friend. 'Don't worry, Neil. I'll take it up with Cowley personally.'

Ignoring them, he went out. There was nothing left here now, and so Bodie and Doyle moved towards the door, having to pass Turvey as they did so. With his drink in his hand, Turvey looked at them. The smile broadened on his face. He took the opportunity to crow over them, flushed with power and victory, confident in his own influence. Mockingly, he lifted the glass to them.

'Sorry you wouldn't join me.'

Bodie halted. He glowered. All his aggressiveness that smouldered so close to the surface and which he could usually, after painful experience, so successfully contain, boiled over.

'Your particularly good Malt Scotch . . . Well, I'll tell you, Mister Turvey, you can take your particularly good Malt Scotch and shove it up your particularly good –'

Bodie's hot words were chopped off as the enraged Turvey hurled the whisky full into his face.

140

Instinctively, Bodie would have thumped him, a chop here, a knee there, a double-hander on the back of his neck as he went down – the red rage roared through him – Doyle had physically to grab Bodie's arm and yank him back.

'*Bodie!*'

Bodie stood, trembling, his face ashen, the whisky dribbling down his forehead and nose and on to his chin. He disdained to lick at it. He fought himself. Then, glaring at Turvey, he managed, with complete disdain, to grind out: 'Good-day, Mister Turvey.'

Doyle got him outside and into the car and sat back, whooshing a gust of air out. That had been a near thing.

By the time they had driven back up to London Sir Frederick Talon had been on the phone to Cowley.

In the bleak offices of C.I.5, with Cowley regarding them as though they had crawled out from under a particularly flat stone, they stood to take their roasting.

'I told you to lay off Turvey. I told you.' Cowley stuck his hands up into the small of his back, and decided against pacing up and down. That damned leg of his had been giving him some rotten gyp just lately. 'I told you. But now. *You* go charging in – against my orders.' He stalked up to Bodie and glared into those dark eyes. 'Are you deaf to what I say? Or are you just plain pig ignorant?'

Doyle admired the old man. He'd gone straight for Bodie. 'Easy on, sir. He just took a glass of Scotch in the face.'

Cowley looked flabbergasted. 'Scotch?'

Doyle amplified the Scotch throwing incident. Bodie finished it by saying: 'Pure Malt. A particularly good Pure Malt Scotch.'

'Then,' said Cowley, 'you're not just deaf. You're stupid. Pure Malt Scotch – on a face like that!'

He turned away, clenched his hands into fists, thinking of the implications, the cunning stratagems, using them, turning back to say in a brisk voice: 'You're angry? Deep down, frustrated, want-to-punch-someone-in-the-face-angry? Yeah. My karate master taught me about anger. Channel it, he

141

said, take it, let it throb up through your body, let it build and grow – and then concentrate it. Let it burst out through your fingers!'

As he finished Cowley brought his rigid hand down in a palm-edge blow that sizzled through the air and stopped a millimetre above the surface of his desk. That was not a karate blow but one of the repertoire of less polite disciplines known to the agents of C.I.5. The effect was electrifying.

Cowley breathed in deeply, limped off to the drinks cabinet, started to pour without a tremble. 'Have a Scotch. It's Malt. And it's pure. For your edification, there is no such thing as a particularly good one. They're all damned good.'

Cowley drank with a great panache, an aplomb. He gestured to the other two drinks he had poured.

'And don't waste it over your face, Bodie. Aim for your throat!'

The crisis was over. The partners knew something of George Cowley and his ways. Thankfully they walked to the drinks cabinet and hoisted their pure Malts.

'Now,' said Cowley, forcefully. 'To concentrate that anger.' He beamed upon them, suddenly benign like a sitting Buddha in an alcove, illuminated by massed candles. 'Files.'

'Files?' Bodie gagged.

'The newspaper files, Bodie. Every word ever written about the Suzy Carter affair.'

'We've been through 'em,' said Doyle.

'A hundred times,' said Bodie.

'Then,' said George Cowley with that suspiciously benign air. 'Make it one hundred and one. Betty has them all laid out for you.' He sipped at his drink, smiling. 'Cheers!'

'And,' said Bodie as they went out. 'That's all that Betty will have laid out for us.'

'You speak for yourself, chum,' said Doyle, and then walked on as fast as his mending limp would allow.

Poor old Bodie – cut up by whisky – and now by a secret fermenting suspicion – it just was not Bodie's day.

Chapter Twelve

The 1953 newspapers yielded a fascinating picture of another time, another life, another world. The Coronation dominated everything, of course; but the sports columns and other news crammed in in tiny squibbets. Doyle and Bodie did as they had been ordered. They spent some time doing just that. The Everest story intrigued them both.

At last Doyle pushed the papers away. The reference office in C.I.5 was just as bleak, just as unwelcoming, as any other of the rooms, apart from operations, communications and the forensics section. Bodie rubbed his eyes and Doyle leaned back wearily.

'It's too damned simple,' said Doyle. 'Turner. Detective Superintendent Turner, suitably bribed, as officer in charge walks right past the man on the door, inside the room, Policewoman Ann Berry, also suitably bribed. Between them they bundle Suzy Carter out of the window – and – '

'Neil Turvey foots the bill?'

'And the whole thing set up by attorney for the defence – *and lately deceased* – Arden French. No case against Turvey. So – case closed.'

Bodie frowned. He sat up. He lowered those daunting eyebrows of his at his partner. 'Say that again.'

'Case closed?'

'No, no. That first bit.' Bodie lifted his hand, sideways on, as though cutting the air before his nose. 'Turner . . . officer in charge . . . '

' . . . walks past the man on the door and – '

Doyle stopped speaking. They looked at each other. Then, on a breath, Doyle said: 'Bodie, we'll make a detective out of you yet.'

George Cowley stayed in his office for just as long as the Terrible Twins stayed in the reference room. Lord Derrington was ushered in by Betty. He looked as calm and dignified as ever, the man at the centre of affairs, a man who had taught Cowley much.

'A wild goose chase, George,' he opened up, sitting down. 'At the time suspicion – *without foundation* – was levelled at Neil Turvey. And now, twenty-five years later, still nothing proven, or ever likely to be. Status quo –'

'Except,' said Cowley in his bleakest manner, 'that I'm now a man short.'

Derrington looked up quickly. 'Oh, yes. Tony Bastable. Yes – sorry to hear about that.'

'Not as sorry as Neil Turvey will be. One day.'

'George!' protested Derrington. 'You can't pursue it. There's nothing to pursue!'

'Perhaps not. But I'll *remember* it – tuck it away –'

'I wish,' said Derrington, touching his fingers to his lips, 'I wish I hadn't opened old wounds in the first place.'

Cowley spoke flatly. 'I'm glad you did.' As Derrington slowly lowered his police fingers, Cowley went on in that ice-flow voice: 'There's someone else, Peter. There *had* to be. Those years ago, Turvey was not in a position to subvert an attorney, a police officer . . . No, there had to be someone else. Someone in authority. A Third Man, if you like.'

At that moment, before Derrington could speak, the door opened. Cowley looked up as the partners entered.

'Yes?'

'The copper, sir,' said Doyle. 'The guard. The man *outside* the door.'

'It took you long enough,' Cowley began, and then saw his two alleged top-agents, and changed that to: 'Now, why didn't *I* think of that?'

'Because,' said Bodie, showing his teeth. '*You* didn't get a Scotch in the face.'

'D'you know who he is?'

'We know who. Frank Hamer. Detective sergeant retired. But not where yet.'

'Get to it, then.' Cowley watched them leave and turned to Derrington, who had listened to all this like a man over-hearing a comic turn in a foreign language. 'Concentration of anger. When it works – ' Cowley chopped his palm-edge down perhaps twenty millimetres. 'It really works!'

'We,' said George Cowley, glaring viciously at Bodie and Doyle, 'are not to blame.' His office lowered down with the shadows clustered in the corners. The battered desk lamp threw a shaft of light which cast Cowley's features into a shadowed devil's mask. He glared up at the partners. 'If Frank Hamer hadn't been off in the wilds of Scotland chasing after stags, we would have found him – in time. Police procedures are effective. In this case – Goddammit – they were too slow.'

'The report from the local police just says he was killed by a shotgun – '

'Stags?'

'His effects are being flown down. Betty – '

'Is at home in bed.' Cowley eyed them. As they were both here before him, he judged Betty was sleeping alone. Although which one – well, that was an inviting conundrum, which one had melted the iceberg.

When the lately deceased Frank Hamer's belongings were brought in to C.I.5 the agents went through them carefully. The statement from Hamer's gillie said that a man had appeared from nowhere and shot Mr Hamer. Poor Mr Hamer. He also added the puzzling remark that Hamer had shot the gunman. Bodie lifted an expensive rifle out of its leather scabbard and held it up. 'Eureka!' he said.

With practised fingers he quickly stripped out the roll of

film from the camera gun. 'If Hamer shot the gunman with this . . . '

'Move it!' snapped Cowley.

Photographics whistled the prints through very fast, still wet, and Cowley and Doyle looked down. Doyle let out a disgusted little puff of sound, a snort of disdain.

'So you know him,' said Cowley, before Doyle could speak.

'Interesting life our boy's led,' observed Bodie. 'Knows some right punks –'

'Sammy Goodman,' said Doyle. 'And, yes, I know him and he is a punk and we will make him cough. That I can guarantee.'

'Can you find him?' demanded Cowley.

'He doesn't know we know. He won't be hiding. We can bring him in.'

Cowley nodded. 'Good.' He looked up, suddenly, sharply. 'And gently, eh? Gently?'

Bodie slammed a fist into his palm. 'Yes, *sir*!'

Doyle armed himself with a sprig of heather and they took an inconspicuous Cortina from the Squad garage. Bodie's Lagonda had been put in for a new windscreen – and that would cost a bomb. They cruised the known haunts of Sammy Goodman. Doyle was working over familiar territory. Goodman was observed leaving a betting shop, looking pleased, openly counting up a wad of fivers. He was that kind of fellow.

'With the three of them – Turner, Berry, Hamer – dead, they must feel secure,' said Doyle as he opened the Cortina's door.

'And Tony,' said Bodie, following him. 'Let us not forget Tony.'

They zeroed in on Goodman and Doyle prodded the heather forward and tickled it under the man's nose, between his face and the fivers.

'Buy some lucky heather?'

Goodman brushed the sprig away impatiently, and looked up ready to blast angrily.

Doyle went on, smiling: 'A sprig of lucky heather. Fresh from the moors of Scotland.'

The wad of fivers exploded from Goodman's palsied hands. The notes flew out, fluttering in the breeze, skittered along the pavement among the shoppers.

Bodie took one arm, Doyle the other.

'You won't need those where you're going, Sammy. Cast thy bread upon the waters – Gotcha!'

The picture taken by Hamer's camera rifle in the instant of his death, as he had sighted and shot at his murderer, showed Sammy Goodman with the shotgun butt pulled into his shoulder. Sammy Goodman remained singularly unimpressed. As he said, the photo could have been taken any time, anywhere, it could have been faked, it wouldn't stand up as evidence.

Bodie and Doyle nodded, sympathetically, and took Goodman for a little cruise around the darkened streets of a particularly mean section of London. The mean streets narrowed about them. The very air breathed of violence. Long featureless brick walls, factory chimneys, railway tracks, cuttings beneath the tracks, the lamp-posts few and far between. The smell of decay and an abandoned sense of isolation made of these mean streets a living hell within the glitter of the metropolis.

Bodie drove and Doyle sat alongside him, half turned, so he could speak easily to Goodman, who sat with one wrist handcuffed up to the passenger grab rail. 'He's very tough,' said Bodie.

'Don't come any tougher.' Doyle nodded, very cheerful.

'I once,' said Bodie. 'Saw an old Gary Cooper movie. They got at this guy through his religion. He wouldn't talk, wouldn't say a word, until they threatened to bury him in a pig-skin.'

Goodman's tough face twitched; but he said nothing.

'Up 'til then,' went on Bodie in that eerie cheerful way, 'Up 'til then he'd been as tough as nails. But the threat of the pig-skin? Then he *really* broke up.'

Doyle looked suddenly sad. 'Wouldn't work with Sammy. He's not scared of anything.' He bent a fierce hard gaze on Sammy Goodman. 'Are you, Sammy?'

'Nothing at all?' said Bodie in a high, incredulous voice.

The Cortina rounded the gas works and started down a narrow road with a corrugated iron fence one side. A few lamps scattered random pools of light. Bodie said: 'But you get my point?' The car hit potholes and jounced. 'Everyone has a room one-oh-one. Something they fear most of all in the whole wide world.'

'Point,' said Doyle, 'taken. Next right.'

The Cortina took the next turning on the right. A sleazy side alley opened up, with a blank brick wall one side and a series of sloped warehouse roofs and walls the other. The car eased to a stop by a lamp-post. This was a mean and nasty area – very mean and exceedingly nasty.

Doyle said to Goodman: 'Room one-oh-one. Know where we are, Sammy? Of course you do. We're in Billy Knowles's area. Billy Knowles? Nasty Billy Knowles – only don't let him hear you say that or he'll have your guts for garters. But it won't be garters. *Or your guts.*'

Sammy Goodman was sweating now, his dark pitted face shining in the lamp's gleam. Doyle regarded him dispassionately.

'You haven't seen Billy in a long while, have you? Not since he warned you off. Told you if he ever saw you in his area again, he'd live up to his name – *Nasty* Billy . . .'

Bodie got out of the car and Doyle unlocked the end of Goodman's handcuffs and dragged him out. He was relatively gentle with him, pace Cowley's orders. They clapped the loose end of the handcuffs around a rusted iron bar cemented into the brickwork. Goodman stood, limp, lax, staring at them. His lower lip showed wet. He shivered.

'Now, Sammy, you have a choice.' Doyle tapped the handcuffs. 'Talk to us, or wait here until Billy arrives. One phone call will have him running all the way.' Doyle moved in. Goodman was now reeking with sweat, a stink on the already foul night air. 'Billy won't work you over. And he won't kill you, either. It'll be somewhere between the two – except, at the end, you'll wish he *had* killed you. You have a choice.'

The partners stared impassively at Goodman. He looked sickly back, shaking, the handcuffs rattling. Then, as he said nothing, they moved back to the car and entered. The engine fired. The Cortina began to roll away . . .

'No!' screamed Sammy Goodman. 'No! *No!*'

The Cortina halted and the doors opened.

Both Bodie and Doyle, in that moment, thought of Tony Bastable and his youthful eagerness.

Cowley waited in his drab office. Not for the first time he had to wrestle with ingrained ideas of justice and truth. If you employ evil means to achieve a good result, do not those evils negate the good? Are you then no better than your enemy? Can ends ever justify the means? All Cowley knew with any certainty was that there were certain moralities for which he fought dourly. Why should the devil have all the good tunes? Why should the Big A, the Action Squad, not fight fire with fire? The reasons were vague and blurred as he sat, thinking of Tony Bastable, thinking of all the good men who had been killed or maimed in the constant struggle against villainy.

Bodie and Doyle came in. They looked not so much tired as though they had gone head-first through the wringer. But they had the penultimate answer.

They told Cowley. They showed him the signed attestation.

Cowley sat back in his old chair.

'Turvey hired him?'

Doyle said: 'Neil Turvey, of Turvey Combines. His contacts remained from his old days of heavy dealing. Goodman's sworn it, attested it, signed it.'

149

'In,' said Bodie. 'Triplicate.'

Cowley felt the doubts slipping away. Evil had to be fought – somehow, by feeble, fragile men.

'So we've got him. We finally nailed Turvey. That just leaves this shadowy Third Man.' Cowley stood up and limped across to the drinks cabinet. He pondered. 'Turvey must have been into this kind of racket up to his neck. He knew just who to go to when he needed muscle – when he needed a hit man. Now, the problem is – who do I send to bring him in? Someone who will treat him with the respect he deserves?'

Bodie and Doyle regarded their chief with sober attention.

'Well, sir,' said Bodie at last. 'We *are* renowned for our kind and sympathetic natures.'

Turvey's lush and palatial home rocked to the sound of high decibel music. The lights spilled out brilliantly from every window. A teenaged crowd danced to the music, drink flowed, the air quivered, the scents wafted mellifluously. Large shiny limousines, and expensive sports cars lined up in the driveway. This was Julia Turvey's eighteenth birthday party, and as the granddaughter of Neil Turvey she could ask for the moon and have it – suitably engraved.

Money, money, money – everywhere in the house and among the guests wealth was displayed with that casual, un-thinking right to possession that marked off these people as among the elect. And, with the money, power and influence.

The music throbbed from a super-high-power hi-fi quad set situated, for the party, in Turvey's study. Speakers blasted the racket out into the lounge and hall and on to the patio where Chinese lanterns glimmered in multi-coloured beauty.

Standing talking to his wealthy neighbours, sleek, polished, laughing people, Turvey was saying: 'Yes, I spoil her, I suppose. But then, why shouldn't I indulge her. She's my only granddaughter, and – ' He stopped, laughing, as Julia leaned over his shoulder and took a quick sip of the drink he held in his white manicured hand.

'Don't worry,' she said, laughing. 'I can hold my liquor.' When she tasted it she made a face. 'Whisky!'

'How's it going in there?'

'Great. Fantastic,' enthused Julia. 'It's a *beautiful* party. Thanks – '

She kissed his cheek lightly and the music stopped in mid-bar.

'Oh!' said Julia, furious. Her brother Mark, a little rumpled from some furtive hand-holding, appeared. He was flushed, very much the upper-crust public-school product, determined to have things his own way. He barged across and disappeared into the study. Teenagers appeared in the doorway of the lounge, laughing and shouting, with a few shrills, looking across to Turvey and his guests and Julia in the hall.

'Come on, Julia! Where's the music! Where did it go! Come on!'

Julia stamped her foot. 'Mark should never have left it – he's supposed to be running the disco – *I'll* fix it!'

Turvey laughed as his granddaughter strutted off to the study. What a girl! He turned back to his guests, smooth, conscious of his position as a powerful man of business, almost patronising, elegantly dignified.

Mark fumbled down behind the set suspecting some dire happenstance. The study was in half-darkness, light spilling in from the open door. A little noise brought Mark up, to stare in bewilderment at a man who stood lazily swinging the plug of the disco equipment. He swung the plug at the end of the lead from side to side, like a pendulum, or a man about to cast a bolas.

Another man leaned against the wall by the windows.

Both these men looked to Mark to be hard – an impression he took more from their stance, their quietness, than from any more strong impression in the half-light.

Julia's silhouette – very fetching – appeared in the lighted rectangle of the door. She was very cross. This was her party and she was so used to having things go the way she wanted

– and her friends would be laughing because the hi-fi equipment she had boasted of had broken down –

'Mark! Will you get it together, and –'

She stopped stock still. She looked into the room and just could not understand what she was seeing.

Bodie swung the plug at the end of the lead.

'The party's over,' he said.

Julia burst out fiercely: 'What! Who are you? Mark – !'

'They came in through the window,' said Mark.

Julia understood now. Her pert face went mean. 'Gate crashers! Well, we'll see about that –'

She swung about, with a little cry of vengeful triumph, as her grandfather walked in, laughing with some jokey remark to his friends outside. Turvey, very much the big man of the moment, said: 'Julia – has the disco equipment – ?'

He saw Doyle and Bodie. He stopped, and the vicious frown of challenged authority began to gather on his face.

Doyle said: 'Good evening, Mr Turvey.'

'How the devil did you get in here?' At Doyle's gesture to the window, Turvey rumbled out: 'You broke in here? You broke into my home!'

Doyle said in a slow, even drawl: 'Well, it was open.'

Turvey started to shake. He felt the fury and the anger and the disgust rising in him. He'd deal with this, and damned quick, too! He lifted his hand, commandingly. 'My god! This is unforgivable! All right, Julia – Mark – I'll attend to this.' He saw them out and they went, sorry that they'd miss the opportunity of seeing their grandfather cut these boors to ribbons. Upstarts!

Turvey swung back to glower at the partners. His anger would have cowed many a man – had done so, in his rise to power and wealth. 'You must be mad, both of you.'

'If,' Bodie pointed out, 'you weren't mad in this job you'd go insane.'

'I'll have you broken for this, smashed, washed up.' Turvey pounced on the phone and wrestled the receiver off, began to dial.

'If you're calling Sir Frederick,' said Doyle, gently. 'He already knows.'

Turvey ignored him, filled with the red fury, went on dialling.

Bodie amplified. He moved closer to Turvey.

'Sir Frederick knows that Sammy talked.'

Turvey finished dialling and stood with the receiver half way to his ear. He heard what this bastard said. He looked. He looked very hard at these two.

Doyle said: 'Sammy Goodman.'

A silence descended as the three stood, held in a stasis and the voice of Sir Frederick Talon sounded tinnily through the receiver. 'Hello ... Hello ... '

Slowly, very very slowly, Turvey replaced the receiver and pushed the phone a little way further on to the desk, fussily. He half-lifted a hand.

'Sammy told us,' Doyle said. 'Told us about Turner – Berry – Hamer – and *you*.'

'So,' said Bodie, briskly. 'It's a murder rap. Hiring him is the same as actually doing it. Means you killed Tony Bastable, too.' Turvey caught the undercurrent in that brisk voice, the depths of feeling being ruthlessly repressed, feelings that were expressed only as: 'We liked Tony.'

Turvey moved back a half-pace. He surveyed them in a fresh light. He made up his mind. 'How much?' said Neil Turvey, a most powerful and influential – and wealthy – man. 'How much? for god's sake, every man has his price – name yours! All I need is one clear hour.'

'Yes. You have a company in South America, don't you?'

'One hour. I'll pay whatever you ask for it.'

In an interested voice, Bodie said: 'Whatever?'

'Yes, yes – '

'In cash?'

'Any currency you name.'

Thoughtfully, Bodie crossed the room past the silent disco equipment to the drinks cabinet. He lifted the bottle he selected – the certain bottle.

'Think I'll sample that pure Malt Scotch now.'

Turvey watched him as a rabbit watches a snake. A life lay in this man's hands. Bodie poured and then stood, looking at the glass. 'Have to admit, Doyle. It's very tempting.'

'Very.'

'And we *could* have been an hour late getting here. Yes – '

Eagerly, taking a step forward, the relief breaking his face from that tense, horrified grimace, Turvey almost babbled. 'Then it's a deal?'

Bodie lifted his head.

'No. Wouldn't be fair to Tony Bastable, would it?' He smiled. 'Tell you what, though – to make up for your disappointment – have a drink on me.'

With a smooth motion Bodie wristed the glass of Scotch full in Turvey's face.

The influential man staggered back, pawing at his face. The whisky shone in the half light. Bodie nodded to Doyle. Doyle stepped across, took Turvey's hand, bent it back, started to clap the cuffs on him. Turvey panicked.

'What are you doing? Handcuffs? You don't need – for pity's sake!' They started to hustle him to the door. 'My family are out there – my granddaughter – her friends – ' He thrust out the handcuffs. The steely glint looked cold. 'Take them off. I'm *begging* you. What kind of men are you?'

Bodie opened the door and as they pushed Turvey out into the bright lights of the hall, Doyle said: 'The kind who catch *your* kind.'

Into the merciless light of the wide hallway Turvey half-stumbled. The two C.I.5 men hustled him along to the door. From the lounge door – the music still dead – the crowd watched. The teenagers stared with shock, Turvey's dignified friends could barely comprehend what was going on. Julia and Mark stood, stunned. No one missed the silver liquid flash of the handcuffs.

The front door opened. For an instant the two hard men appeared there, their prisoner between them; then they were gone.

154

Only then could Julia take a stricken step forward. She tottered. She could not understand.

'Grandfather!' Then, in a rising wail: '*Grandpa!*'

George Cowley often considered ways and means of improving the Action Squad, the Big A. He personally selected the best men he could find. But he could never hope to winnow all the fields himself. He made it known that he didn't give a damn for almost anything his men did provided they retained that essential respect for worthwhile humanity and came up with the answers. Sometimes, he felt, sometimes, he ought to have been a monk. He always took things so damn personally.

He threw the documents he had been studying for the hundredth time back on to the cluttered desk and leaned back. He felt sad and weary – and they were sins to a man who was not a monk but the chief of an Action Squad empowered to look into any and every transgressions of the laws of the land. And those that transgressed unwritten laws, also ...

He opened a drawer and took out a gun. It was not a particularly noteworthy handgun in many respects, if compared to the flash handguns these youngsters sported. But it had served him well in the past. It was a damned great cannon, a .455 Webley, long since superseded in British Army service. But there were few handguns to match it for accuracy and very very few anywhere near in stopping power. He checked it with a smooth competent action that told of years of experience. He didn't often use it now. Usually he took along a snubnose. He shut the gun and hesitated – then placed it carefully back in the drawer.

He stood up and went across to the rack and put on his light topcoat. Back at the desk he picked up an old newspaper and folded it carefully, placed it in his topcoat pocket. He had arranged to meet up at the most suitable place. But he felt a strange reluctance actually to start to go there.

He moved to the door. He stopped, and looked back at

his desk. He stood for some time, his head just that little bit on one side, the overhead light glinting on his sandy hair.

Then, purposefully, he crossed to the desk, drew out the drawer, picked up the gun, slid it into his pocket. It weighed half a ton. But he was used to carrying weight, was George Cowley.

Events moved in cycles, from the cosmic scale down to the miniscule scale of mere human beings. Cowley walked along the dusty corridor of the Star Hotel. The bulldozers would be in very soon now – so when that would be was anybody's guess – but the dusty, dank, mouldering feel of the place exactly matched his mood.

Bodie and Doyle, obeying his instructions after they had stowed Turvey away safely, walked towards him along the corridor. Truth to tell, he barely saw them. He marched straight past. Both his hands were thrust deeply into his topcoat pockets.

The partners looked after him, little frowns dinting in above their noses; then they looked at each other, and turned, without a word being necessary, and walked slowly along after their chief.

Cowley went into the room along the corridor – that fatal room – and went across to the window. He stood, hunched, staring down at the ground. Twenty-five years ago a young defenceless girl had hurtled down all that awful drop to her death.

Perhaps, now, back in that same room, this was some kind of jubilee for her, of belated recompense for Suzy Carter – although that was nonsense. You couldn't recompense someone for their death. Avenge – you could avenge – and that was more often than not not worth the candle. But, here and now, a kind of justice had to be done. It was part and parcel of the ethics of C.I.5, one of the reasons they existed, a task set to the hands of Cowley and his men and no nonsense about obeying orders without question.

Standing looking out of the window, his back to the room

– standing as Suzy Carter must have been standing all those jubilee twenty-five years ago, vulnerable, fragile, ready for the savage thrust that would spin her brutally out to her death – Cowley heard the door open and the measured footsteps crossing the empty, dusty floor. The floorboards creaked. He waited until the newcomer was almost upon him, waited coolly, waited with the absolute conviction that he had to do what he was going to do and that to do otherwise would mean he might as well pack up shop and disband C.I.5 altogether.

At precisely the right moment, Cowley said: 'You know why I asked you to meet me here?'

The footsteps stopped. The creaking floorboards fell silent.

Cowley turned. He was not exactly smiling; but the hurt caught up his lip, gave him the semblance of a grimace that might have been construed as a smile – by someone who did not know him.

'The scene of the crime.'

A tiny wind blew down the alley outside. A lick of wind whispered through the windows, lifting scraps of browned paper, pugging the dust. Footprints showed in the dust, soft-edged, fluffy, many footprints; but the dust persisted, the dust remained.

'You didn't tell me the good news,' went on Cowley, still with that fixed grimace that was not a smile on his creased face. His vowels had never been plummier. 'That you're being considered as the new party leader. Means you could actually be Prime Minister one day, Peter. You could have been.'

Lord Derrington stood facing Cowley, not smiling, his mouth a trifle pursed, his eyes puzzled, waiting.

Cowley did not take his hands from his pockets. 'I killed Suzy Carter.' Sir Arden's dying words, and they panicked you into testing just how good the cover up was all those years ago. Panicked you into finding out just how safe you were. And you used my organisation to do it. That was a bad mistake, Peter.'

157

'Turvey?' Derrington spoke quietly but perfectly in control.

'No. No, Turvey hasn't talked. He never will. He's lost his liberty; but he's damned sure going to try and hold on to his Company. If he implicated you – that would go, too. No, I didn't need Turvey to talk. I can still put two and two together and come up with four. Just took me a little longer this time – because I trusted you – because it was unthinkable.'

Cowley moved his head, just a little, but the gesture seemed like a thunderclap in that empty, dusty, memory-laden room.

'You were that third man.'

Derrington just stood, regarding Cowley with interest.

'What will you do?'

'You betrayed my trust – but that can happen – that's forgivable – barely.' Cowley seemed more remote, now, as though he had cleared some personal obstacle, climbed some private mountain of doubt and self-mistrust, of awe and of probity. Now he felt the freedom, the freedom of having scaled the heights despite his own misgivings. He could look down, now, down upon the world spread out below, look down in humility, knowing he had climbed his own private mountain and climbed out of hell in the scaling of that peak.

'But you were also responsible for the death of one of my men. That, I can never forgive.'

As though Lord Derrington recognised the change in Cowley – although he could never understand that sense of having scaled a mountain and reached the summit and so burst through into freedom – he stared for a long instant at the Chief of C.I.5 and then began a small but completely overt move towards the door.

He moved with purpose towards the door and escape. And as he moved so he began to take his hand from the pocket of his coat.

Quick – yes, very, very quick – the old Webley .455 appeared in Cowley's hand. Derrington blinked. Such a big

158

gun, and yet such speed in the draw . . .

Derrington halted instantly, and his hand dropped something back into his pocket.

'I think,' Cowley told him. 'I really think I'd like you to try and run, Peter, to shoot your way out. So I could gut-shoot you!'

'You wouldn't use that, George. Not on me.'

Was there a perceptible movement again, a flexing of the immaculately-clad knee, the suggestion of a move towards the door?

With the big Webley rock-steady, Cowley said: 'Try me.'

A voice floated in the open door – Doyle's voice.

'Then, afterwards, try us!'

The partners lounged in. They were not smiling. The time for foolishness of that nature was long over. Tony Bastable and Suzy Carter and all the others time ago. Doyle held his S.&W. .357 Magnum, and Bodie his 9mm Browning Hi-Power.

Cowley suddenly scowled at them, back to the routine of daily life with the Big A.

'I don't need your help!'

Bodie said: 'Not here to help, sir. Just to pick up a few tips.'

Cowley waited for perhaps two heartbeats. Then he twinkled the big old Webley back into his topcoat pocket. He advanced on Derrington, and stood, looking eye to eye. Bodie and Doyle had no real idea what the chief was thinking, feeling, nothing of scaling mountains . . . Then: *'Take him!'*

Bodie and Doyle gripped Derrington's shoulders. They turned him, started to lead him away. They were professionals. Every inch professionals. Derrington knew that, he could feel it by that light yet firm pressure on his shoulders, smell it in the musty air, see it in those two handguns so casually gripped ready for instant action.

Derrington turned back. His face twisted. 'George?'

Cowley turned his back.

He walked slowly back to the window, stood looking out and down.

Again, Derrington called, appealing, pleading as Bodie and Doyle led him away. 'George!'

Cowley looked down the drop. Suzy Carter had tumbled down there. Twenty-five years ago. He turned when the room and the corridor were silent once more. He moved away from that sheer drop. As he went he took the old folded newspaper from his pocket and let it drop on to the warped floorboards, dusty, marked with footprints, bare.

The yellowed paper flapped open. Black headlines showed as sharp as ever.

EVEREST CONQUERED.

Cowley walked slowly from the room, back to C.I.5, back to the Action Squad, back to the Big A.

Twenty-five years ago Everest had also been conquered.